Freya's Freedom

The Tower and The Eye, Volume 3

Kira Morgana

Published by Teigr Books, 2024.

This story is dedicated to all the Dancers out there - may you be the power in your own story.

Chapter One

The sunset flooded over the Galivorian Mountains, the jagged shadows piercing the foothills. Sheep being herded toward their winter pastures bleated in panic as the wind blew the scent of hunting Direwolves over them from the nearby forest; the trees flaming in their autumn colours.

To the west of Jirshan, the spear of I'Mor Barad rose to stab the rose and orange tinted sky and the flare of scarlet light at the top of the tower spattered like blood drops onto the bleak granite mountains surrounding it.

The tarnished gold throne sat alone on the dais, its usual occupant stood in front of an eastern facing window, watching as a voluptuous young woman with long black hair and deep green eyes, kissed the wrinkled merchant whose knee she sat on.

The Jar beside the throne coughed.

"Um, Lord? Should she not be leaving?"

The Aracan Katuvana snapped his fingers and the picture of Jetara; the Mistress of the Pleasurehouse sprang to life in the top corner.

"Yes, My Master." The woman's face was sullen.

"Why is the girl still with you? Are you trying to anger our Lord?" the Jar snapped.

"No, Master! She did accept her freedom and the gold you did bid me give her. The Merchant came in as she was leaving and did ask her to stay with him," the Pleasure House Keeper wailed. "When I did try to make her leave, she told me to no interfere as she was a free woman and could do as she saw fit." Jetara's face crumpled and tears flowed.

The Jar remained silent, but its single eye looked up at the watching man.

The Aracan grunted and snapped twice.

"The Aracan Katuvana has decreed you are innocent in this matter. Leave the girl be and accord her what hospitality she asks for... for free." The Jar paused.

"Yes! Yes, my Lord. Jetara shall do as Jetara is commanded." Jetara wiped her eyes with the end of her silk headscarf, and then blew her nose on it.

Disgusting baggage. The Jar shuddered at the woman's actions. *Such women are not fit to be in charge of anything more than a scullery.*

"See that you do." It growled.

The Aracan Katuvana snapped his fingers once and Jetara's picture disappeared. He spun around and returned to his throne, resting his head against the throne back.

"I shall keep a watch upon the Girl, Lord. Sleep well," the Jar said as a faint snore emerged from under the hood. The Jar's gaze turned back to the scene on the window.

BEING FREE ISN'T AS good as I thought it would be Freya mused as she trudged up the north-west road. *Yes, I no longer have to do everything that I am told. True, I have my own money. Nevertheless, none of the older slaves at the Pleasurehouse told me being so well known in the Capital would be such a problem.* She sighed and stopped for a moment, putting her bag down and rolling her shoulders. *I wish I had taken that Merchant up on his offer. Then I could have ridden in a carriage to meet...*

"And what is a sweet young maiden such as yourself doing afoot?" a voice asked from behind her.

The interruption of her thoughts startled her for a moment before she turned and shaded her eyes from the morning sun.

Down the Reldierholm road, on a pure white mare, rode an Elf. He wore a green and white tabard over his travelling clothes and led a packhorse as well as a high-stepping coal black Elven stallion.

He'd have to be at least a knight, and a wealthy one to afford such animals. Freya dropped into her sultry, smooth 'work' voice, tilting her head to the right. At the same time, she felt for the hilt of her dagger, just in case.

"I have not money enough to purchase a steed nor carriage, Sir Knight."

He reined to a halt beside her and dismounted, flourishing his cloak.

"Where is your escort? A pure and beauteous maiden such as yourself should not roam the wilds of Jinran unescorted."

"My brother, Sir Grald, is meeting me in Jinra, Sir Knight. The message he sent assured me that I would be unmolested in my travel." Freya emphasised the words carefully and gauged the effect they were having on the Elf, adding a little flutter of her long black eyelashes as punctuation.

"Sir Grald? I know no Knight of that name or even Paladin such as I," he replied.

"He has only late come to the honour, Sir." She sighed and sank to the ground.

"Fair Maid? Is there something wrong?" He knelt beside her.

"I left Jira late last night and I have been walking since," she told him, raising one hand to her mouth in a fake yawn.

In fact, she had left Jira just before daybreak. The rigours of her 'Profession' had required her to stay in good shape and she was not as frail as she looked, so the walk from Jira to the junction of the Reldierholm Road had taken her just over two hours.

The Paladin gasped.

"That is a goodly way for one of your gentle demeanour to have paced. You must be exhausted."

She sighed and looked up at him through her eyelashes, making sure to take a deep breath before she spoke. His gaze flicked to her chest, then with obvious difficulty, he looked away again.

"Sir Paladin, you are once again right in your summation. I was about to take a rest when you chanced upon my path." *Men are so easy to manipulate. They only see the outer form and make assumptions based on your looks.* She let out a long breath with a tired blink.

"Then allow me to make your rest more comfortable." He hobbled his horses and bustled around her.

He started a fire, set up an awning and laid out a cloth, adding a few flat cushions under it. Then he helped her across to the awning, brought her small bag of belongings to her and within ten minutes, he had made her some tea.

"In truth I also needed to rest myself and my horses. I have lately come from Laikholm." He turned back to the fire and poured himself a cup. Then he set a copper pot over the fire, adding various ingredients from another bag.

Soon the steam rising from the pot wafted a scent over them and set Freya's stomach rumbling, so to distract herself, she studied the design on the back of his pristine Tabard.

She recognised the Tree of Espilieth surmounted by the Crown of Alethdariel. *The tree means he's a Paladin of Espilieth and the crown with one gem means he's one of the Princes of Alethdariel. Not sure what the Eye on a Staff is.*

"May I enquire as to your identity, Sir Paladin?" she ventured, breaking the silence.

"Please forgive me, sweet maiden. I am remiss in my courtesy." He stood, turned and bowed with a small flourish. "I am Sir Vrenstalliren of Alethdariel, a Paladin of Espilieth and Son of the Queen. And yourself?" reestablishing his position before the hearth, he retrieved another pan and began doing something else.

"I am Freya of Jira," she replied absently, her nose detecting bacon... and something else. *Garlic? Oh, I haven't had garlic for a long time. Not since...* her thoughts trailed away as the Paladin set a plate of fried bacon, stewed mushrooms and waybread before her.

Her stomach gave an audible rumble and she winced, hoping he would ignore it.

"I hope this meagre fare shall still the hunger within, Lady Freya of Jira." He sat across from her with a similar plateful.

Phew. Freya let the title slide. *It won't hurt if he thinks I'm a noble... I hope.*

They ate with no more conversation, a fact that Freya was thankful for. *I have no idea how I am going to answer any more questions beyond what I already have.* Then the elf cleared up the camp and brought his white mare over to Freya. She took the reins and allowed him to help her mount.

"We will attempt to find you a suitable steed in the next town, Lady Freya. I cannot ride Ohtár for longer than a few hours. He is a little sensitive." He said as he mounted his Charger.

Freya eyed the big black horse with unease. Although she was an excellent equestrian having been trained by one of her first regular customers, War Stallions needed a firm hand and Ohtár seemed more than a little sensitive. He rolled his eyes whenever so much as a fly came near him.

I'm certainly not touching him, Freya thought. She gently patted the white mare's neck and was rewarded with a gentle nuzzle. *This girl is a lady, even if I'm not.*

A couple of hours later, just outside Jiren, the packhorse disturbed a pheasant in the grass at the side of the road. The mare and the packhorse didn't react, but Ohtár reared and pawed the air.

When he came down, he disturbed a small rocky mound at the side of the road, stones tumbling across the grass and dirt. The afternoon light glinted off a hard polished surface and it caught Freya's attention.

"What's that?" she slipped off the mare and as the Paladin calmed Ohtár down, unearthed a small chest-like box.

"'Tis a pretty thing, Freya." Vrenstalliren said, dismounting.

"It's made of red Graistun from my country," she replied absently. "It's usually only used for magical or precious items."

"The box appears seamless, how would one open such a thing without magic?" The Paladin peered over her shoulder.

Straightening up, she brushed dirt from the gold inlay surrounding an enamelled crest and frowned. "That's my great grandfather's crest, but what is one of his treasure boxes doing so far from Elysia?" she muttered.

"Elysia? I thought you were from Jira?"

Damn, Freya thought, *I didn't mean to say that aloud. Now what do I do?* She thought quickly.

"My family stretches far afield, Sir Paladin, my parents came to Jira before I was born." She opened it, gently touching the gems on the crest. *I think that's the pattern Mama used to use on hers. I never did understand why she brought it with her. Grald said it was because Papa told her to, but it never rang true to me when he said it.* The lid opened and she picked up a smaller gold container reverentially.

"That container alone would be worth a small fortune; enough to buy a fair estate from the Council of Thirteen, m'lady."

"It's worth far more than that to me. It's an heirloom of my family, but how it got here I have no idea." She frowned and put the gold container back, closed the box and put it into her bag. *More to the point, it looked like my mother's ring box. Grald took it with him when he left to find work, so why is it here? I'll look inside when I get a chance.*

"Shall we continue on to Jiren?" Vrenstalliren asked, mounting Ohtár again.

She nodded, swinging herself up into the saddle with practised ease.

"Let's go."

As they started up the road again, Freya sighed. *Thank the Gods of Light that Lord Southnra and I went riding a few days ago, or I would be so sore right now that I wouldn't be able to ride.*

Chapter Two

There was only one tavern in Jiren. It was so opulent that Freya did a double take as she walked in.

"I never expected to see something like this outside of Jira," she said to Vrenstalliren.

The Paladin shrugged.

"'T'is but an Inn."

"The Golden Dice is famed throughout Jinran, Sweet Lady." The tavern keeper stepped out from behind the bar and swept a bow. "I am Master Groilin. Might I enquire if you will be needing rooms?"

"I thank you for your concern, Master," Freya replied briskly. "We shall indeed."

Vrenstalliren raised an eyebrow at her but followed her lead. "Two rooms to be precise. I am the Lady's Guardian and will need to be close by."

"May I request the pleasure of your names for the records of my business?" Master Groilin moved back to the bar and opened a ledger.

"I am Sir Vrenstalliren of Alethdan, and you have the honour of hosting Lady Freya of Elysina," the elf answered.

Freya took the change of name without blinking. *I wonder what he's playing at; he's obviously worked out that I'm not what I told him I was, but if he was angry, surely, he would have confronted me about it before we got here...*

The tavern keeper wrote their names into his ledger and selected a pair of keys from the rack behind him.

"I will show you to your rooms; I have just the thing for a Lady and her Guardian."

THE TRAVELLER ENTERED the main square warily, keeping his hood up and sticking to the lengthening shadows. The few townsfolk he encountered took one look at his stocky form, the dark grey-green skin of his hand and the skull headed staff that he carried, before hurrying away as fast as they could.

"It would appear no one wishes to make your acquaintance, Kraarz."

The traveller's companion strode along behind him; hand on the hilt of a long slim bladed sword.

"More likely they are scared off by your scars, Lin," he grunted.

"Still, it keeps the streets clear for our search."

"I told you, Lin. The spirits told me that we would find the Empress amongst dice of gold," the traveller growled out.

"Kraarz, I still don't understand why you are doing this. Returning the Empress to Elysia is my task." His companion stopped in the light from a house window.

"You saved my life, Lin. Those who I had once called family would have torn me apart, had you not intervened. The Spirits told me to aid you." Kraarz shook his head and continued to walk.

"So where are these dice of gold, Kraarz?" Lin followed him, looking around exaggeratedly.

"There." Kraarz pointed his staff at the tavern in front of them. "I can feel the presence of the Empress within."

"How...? No, don't tell me. The Spirits, right?" Lin sighed. "I just hope they'll let us inside."

"You must go within. I shall return to the outskirts and camp, while you persuade her to return with you," Kraarz told her. "As you have seen before, humans are not comfortable with my kind."

"Kraarz, I would prefer it if you stayed here, where I can defend you if need arises." The warrior frowned. "Stay here, I'll be back in a minute."

Kraarz sat down on the bench outside. "I understand. I shall wait here until you tell me to go."

LIN PUSHED OPEN THE door and stepped into the crowded common room. The scent of refined incense mingled with wine and mead. All around her, people gambled and drank. In one corner, a girl wearing a blue silk robe and silver bells danced on a dais with a white snake. The Tavern Keeper stood behind the bar. He polished glasses and watched the room, while several well-endowed women served the drinks.

Surely, the Empress wouldn't be in this place. It may be well kept, but it is more a Pleasurehouse than an Inn. Lin frowned and her expression cleared a path through the crowd before her.

The Tavern Keeper saw her, put his polishing cloth down and left the bar, moving his bulk through the crowd easily.

Lin moved forward to meet him.

"Welcome to the Golden Dice, my Lady." The man bowed. "I am Master Groilin, the proprietor. May I enquire as to your needs this fine evening?"

Lin looked at him, staying silent. *We need to rest properly and if she is here, we will not find her by leaving again. However, will this man allow Kraarz inside?*

Master Groilin tilted his head to one side.

"My Lady?"

"I have a companion outside that many of your profession would not allow under their roofs," Lin said. "I could not stay in such places because of such rudeness and would not stay without him. Are you afflicted with this problem?"

Groilin blinked, obviously working his way through the sentence. While he was considering it, the door banged open, and a man rushed in.

"There're Urakhs in town!" he yelled.

Several men swivelled round and stared at the newcomer. Lin watched him as he approached the bar.

"Pah! You and your stories, Andren," one of the women behind the bar snorted. "There hasn't been an Urakh incursion in Jinran since before the Black Tower War!"

"I'm telling you it's true. I saw 'im with me own two eyes," Andren said.

The woman rolled her eyes to the ceiling.

"Andren Farmsmith, you always say that. What of that Direwolf Pack you saw, with your own two eyes, out beyond Stiller's mill? The Ranger investigated and he says they found nought, but white fox prints."

"Peace, Leilian," Groilin said with a half smile. "Give the man a rest from your tongue."

Lin came to an abrupt decision.

"There is indeed an Urakh in town," she said.

The room fell quiet, and every face turned to look at her.

"He is with me," she told them. "He is my travelling companion and has aided me many times."

"That's what you meant, isn't it?" Groilin asked her. "You wanted to know if he would be allowed in."

"It is. We have travelled for many days from the Empire together," Lin replied, sweeping her eyes around the room and counting those who had weapons. "Since crossing into Jinran, only a handful of inns and taverns have allowed him into their buildings."

"Where is he then?" Andren demanded, his hand gripping the hilt of a long dagger, the blade winking with lamplight as he trembled.

"If you did not see him, then he did not want to be seen," Lin smiled faintly. "He has many powers and can do much good for those who do not harm him."

A mutter of unease rippled through the common room.

"He's a Shaman?" Leilian whispered.

Lin heard her clearly and nodded.

Master Groilin surveyed the faces in the room and took a deep breath.

"Bring the gentlesir in."

Several of the men stood up, hands on their swords; Andren snarled wordlessly and took a step forward.

"I am a Master Tavern Keeper. It is against the creed of my profession to keep a potential customer in the chill of an autumn night, when I have a room and food available." Groilin glared at all the men who held their swords. "There will be no violence against my guests and any who do insult them so, will find themselves banned from the Golden Dice!"

The men all sat down again, including the farmhand, who continued to stare angrily at Master Groilin.

Groilin smiled at Lin, "Bring your companion within, my Lady."

Lin went to the door and opened it. Kraarz still sat on the bench, his hood pulled low over his eyes.

"You can come in now."

The Urakh looked up at her.

"You are sure that I am welcome?"

"The Tavern Keeper has reassured me of that fact." She placed one hand on his shoulder.

"Then it would be rude of me to wait any longer." Kraarz stood up and Lin moved back slightly, dropping her arm to allow the Shaman to enter.

The common room was silent as Kraarz stepped in. He pulled down his hood and the tall red ponytail atop his head sprang upright, the black and white feathers that decorated it dropping on their leather thongs to trail down Kraarz's shoulders.

Lin shut the door behind them and followed Kraarz as he used his staff to find his way forward to where Groilin stood.

"Master Groilin, allow me to introduce Kraarz Spiritcaller of the Northern Urakh Tribe. Kraarz, this is Master Groilin, the owner of the Golden Dice," Lin said.

Kraarz bowed low.

"Master Groilin. We Urakhs never accept shelter without providing a useful guest gift." When he rose, he held out a hand. In the greeny-grey scaled hand lay a tiny gold pot with an emerald encrusted lid. "I am afraid that this is a mere trifle in comparison with what I could once provide, but I am sure that you will find it useful."

Groilin took the pot.

"A trifle? This is an exquisite work of art, Kraarz." He turned it carefully

"'Twas crafted by my cousin. The real value is not the gaudy gems and gold on the outside, but the powder within." Kraarz grinned, showing rows of pointed teeth. "A small pinch in your ale start at brewing time will produce ferment so fine that even the Gods shall envy you."

"That is a princely gift indeed. I shall treasure the container and use the powder sparingly. Ale that can produce jealousy in the Gods may be a dangerous substance!" Groilin laughed.

Lin frowned. *Is he trying to upset Kraarz?* She tensed, her hand rising to her belt and the sword that hung from it.

The Urakh Shaman laid one hand on Lin's arm.

"Calm yourself, Lin. Master Groilin means what he says. This I know."

Lin dropped her hand to her side.

"So, two rooms with meals?" Groilin bustled towards the bar. As he moved, several of men left the common room, muttering about getting up early. Andren was one of them, sliding past Lin and Kraarz with his lips pulled back from his teeth in a snarl.

"Andren! You didn't pay for your drink," Leilian called after him.

"You can keep your stinking ale. I ain't drinkin' in a Tavern that harbours monsters under their roof," Andren stopped to shout back.

"Then, as there aren't any more Taverns in this town, you had best move, Andren," Groilin spun and snapped at the man. "For you are banned from the Golden Dice from this moment on."

Andren hawked and spat on the polished wood floor.

"This Urakh will bring trouble upon us, you wait and see."

"Out!" Groilin roared.

Andren left the tavern and slammed the door behind him. Groilin looked at Leilian.

"How much does he owe, wife?"

"His tab stands at four gold, Groilin," the woman replied.

The tavern keeper sighed.

"I will have to visit his master in the morning to arrange a repayment schedule."

"'Tis a goodly sum for a farmhand," Kraarz noted. "Here, I shall extend a magnanimous offer and pay his bill." He put four large gold Elysian coins into Groilin's hand.

Groilin blinked at the coins.

"These are Elysian Half-Marks. One of those be sufficient for that vagabond's drinks."

"Then take the others to cover our stay under your roof," Kraarz grinned.

Chapter Three

The next morning after a leisurely bath, Freya dressed and went down to the common room with the intention of getting some breakfast. *Porridge, honey and a little watered wine will do, I think.*

Vrenstalliren had insisted on a private dining room last night, but while Freya found him charming, it had been boring just listening to him boast about his exploits. *Thank Ailliana and her stories that I am used to doing that sort of thing.*

The common room was empty, and Freya slipped into a seat by the fire, relishing the heat from the glowing embers.

"Ah, Lady Freya. You grace my common room with your presence. I hope you slept well." Groilin appeared in the door from the kitchen.

"I did, thank you." Freya smiled as the Tavern Keeper approached.

He sat down opposite her.

"I hope I am not being forward, but is there any chance of you performing tonight?"

Freya blinked in consternation for a moment; then she laughed.

"You've seen me before, haven't you?"

"It took me a while to recognise you, but before I married and gained this Tavern with my Mastery, I worked for Jetara as her assistant." Groilin smiled wistfully, "When you danced, the whole room would watch."

"I remember you now; I used to call you Gremlin." Freya giggled. "I was a mere child. Dancing was the only thing I could do."

Groilin laughed. "Is your favourite breakfast still porridge and honey?"

Freya nodded. "That's what I was going to order."

"Then I shall assemble it now." He stood up.

As Master Groilin went into the kitchen, Freya watched an odd couple of travellers enter the common room.

One was a strange grey-green skinned creature with sharp peg teeth, a tall red ponytail on the top of his head and pure white eyes. Despite his drab, mud stained clothing and quiet demeanour, the creature made Freya shiver with fear.

The other traveller, a woman, wore bright blue silk tunic with matching soft leather trousers. The tunic was embroidered with a silver wingless dragon that Freya recognised but couldn't place.

Why does that woman's clothing make me feel so sad? she wondered

"Aha, Lady Freya. I trust you slept well." Vrenstalliren's voice boomed through the room and Freya plastered her face with a soft smile.

"I did, Sir Paladin, thank you."

The elven Paladin wore soft leather hunting garb and carried a longbow and quiver.

"I decided that my armour was far too conspicuous to escort you properly within the town, so I have changed to something more appropriate."

He certainly looks far more handsome like this. Freya mused, as she looked him over.

"Good idea, Sir Paladin. I'm going shopping after breakfast for something a bit more practical to wear."

He inclined his head and smiled.

"I shall accompany you in that endeavour. Another night's rest here will suit my mounts perfectly, and I have need to find you a mare."

"I would appreciate the help." Freya smiled and batted her eyelashes. "I am a good horsewoman, but my experience of buying animals is not in league with my riding skills."

The Paladin laughed and sat down as Groilin brought out Freya's breakfast.

"Did I hear you say that you needed a mount, Lady Freya?" the Tavern Keeper said as he placed the bowl down in front of her.

Freya nodded as she scooped up a spoonful of honeyed porridge.

"I need a horse that will be able to carry me steadily, and for a goodly distance as I am meeting my brother in Jinra."

"I shall send a runner to the best Livery Stable in town. Merely mention my name and Master Hedlan shall provide all that you will need." Master Groilin said. "Now Sir Paladin, what would you have for breakfast?"

ACROSS THE ROOM, KRAARZ smiled.

"The lady you are seeking is with the elf."

Lin scanned the room, allowing her eyes to rest a moment or two longer on the exotic looking, dark haired woman beside the fire.

"She has the correct features and colouring, Kraarz, but there is more to being Empress than that."

"Yes. We will have to accompany her on her journey. The spirits have told me as much." The Urakh used his staff to attract the Tavern Keeper's attention. "That will give you time to get to know her."

The Tavern Keeper came across to their table.

"Good Morrow, honoured Guests. May I fulfil your breakfast requirements?"

"Master Groilin, I would appreciate some milk and fruit if you will." Kraarz said.

Groilin nodded and looked at Lin.

"Would you like anything, my Lady?"

"I'll have tea, bread and honey, thank you." She paused, "Tell me, Master Groilin; what do you know of the lady with the elven warrior?"

"Lady Freya? She is from the city of Jira, our capital city." Groilin frowned. "Why do you wish to know?"

Lin sensed that he was reluctant to talk about her.

"My Mistress sent me to find someone who appears very similar in looks to this lady. Would you introduce me? I mean no harm to her."

"I will inform Lady Freya of your request. It will be her decision," Groilin said. "One of my girls will bring you your food."

HAVING BOUGHT VARIOUS items of clothing and other travel fripperies from the stalls in the Market, Freya and Vrenstalliren made their way to what Master Groilin had assured them was the finest Horse Dealer in the area.

Vrenstalliren strode ahead of Freya, enumerating the many horse companions he'd had since he started riding.

Freya followed him with only half a mind on his story. *Why are that woman's clothes so familiar to me? It's as if I've seen them before, but somewhere else.* Out of the corner of her eye, she saw a flash of bright blue. *I'm seeing things now. Concentrate, Freya.*

"Here we are!" Vrenstalliren stopped in front of a large barn with a sign bearing a rearing stallion on it.

"That's good." Freya looked around. *Is someone following me? I feel like I'm being watched.* There were plenty of people around, but no one seemed to be paying any attention to her or the Paladin.

"Welcome to The Black Stallion Livery Stables!" a voice boomed out, preceding a mountain of a man who strode out of the barn. "If you are in the market for a mount, you did come to the right place. I am Hedlan, the owner."

Vrenstalliren stepped forward.

"I am Sir Vrenstalliren of Alethdan, Guardian of Lady Freya. We find ourselves in need of a mount for Lady Freya and..."

"Yes, I did speak to Master Groilin's runner. He apprised me of the Lady's need," Hedlan waved the elven Paladin silent. "I have four mounts out back that may suit her."

Vrenstalliren blinked and looked at Freya as the man beckoned them to follow.

"The Tavern Keeper knows you?"

Freya blushed.

"Master Groilin knew me when I was a child, but I only realised the connection this morning."

Vrenstalliren frowned but said nothing as they followed Hedlan through the barn.

Freya breathed in the sweet, pungent aroma of hay and horses, the air full of straw dust, turning the morning light into deep golden beams. *The stables were always my favourite place, even before I went to Jira.*

At the other end of the barn, double doors opened out onto a sand floored ring. Four horses stood with their grooms; two bays, one albino and the other pure black. Freya felt a childlike surge of joy force its way up.

"They're beautiful."

Vrenstalliren made a show of walking around all four, examining their conformation, hooves and teeth.

"They are adequate," he sniffed.

An audience had gathered around the ring and Freya spotted the woman in blue and the strange creature who accompanied her. He wore a brown hooded robe now, but her skin crawled at his look.

To hide her unease, Freya approached the first bay. She looked him over.

"He's a gelding?"

The groom nodded.

Placing one hand on his withers, she vaulted onto the gelding's back. After trotting him around the ring, she dismounted and shook her head.

"He has an uncomfortable gait. Take a look at his offside fore, he was favouring it."

"Damn stablehands know nothing of such things." Hedlan glared at the groom, who checked the horse's leg and nodded back at his master. "Send for the Farrier immediately." The groom acknowledged the order as he took the horse back into the barn

She tried the second bay, a mare this time, who attempted to unseat her. Freya laughed and kept her place.

"Spirited, but I don't think we'd get on." She dismounted and held her hand out to the horse. The mare snapped at her. "See? She can smell my Guardian's stallion and considers me a threat to her chances."

Taking one long look at the albino, Freya shook her head.

"Her breathing is laboured, just standing still. I think someone took you for a ride with this one, Hedlan."

Hedlan took a closer look at the mare and growled.

"You do be right, Lady. I did not buy this one, she was a debt payment."

"She's in foal though; you might make your money back," Freya said, surprising herself. *How did I know that?*

The Livery Owner ran his hand gently down the mare's barrel.

"Hmm. Take her to the breeding yard," he said to the groom who had returned from returning the bay mare to her stall. "Be careful and do no spook her."

The groom took the mare away, talking quietly to her.

Freya stepped up to the black. She looked him in the eye and smiled.

The horse whickered softly and extended his nose to her. He stamped one hoof, the feathers that covered his hooves tickling Freya's legs.

"What's his name?" she asked, stroking the soft nose.

"He do be Korariettln. The fellow I bought him from claimed he had Elvish blood."

Vrenstalliren looked the black over more carefully.

"He may be right. He has a similar conformation to Ohtár."

"Black Spring Magic." Freya smiled. "I like it." She mounted and took him in a circle around the ring. *He's gorgeous.*

"My Dam was Elvish. My Sire, an Each Usage from Galivor. I like you, can I come with you?" The horse asked her in a strong smooth voice that echoed through her mind.

Freya jumped a little.

"You can talk?" she whispered, not wanting to lose any face in front of the Horse Dealer.

"Only to you. Everyone else around here is too closed minded, even that Elven Paladin." Korariettln snorted. *"Reply to me by thinking your words rather than speaking them."*

Freya patted his neck and followed his instruction.

"Then you shall come with me." She dismounted gracefully. "I'll take him. How much?"

"He's still a Stallion, Lady. It is unseemly for a maiden to ride a Stallion." Vrenstalliren burst out.

Freya turned on him.

"You overstep your bounds, Sir Paladin. I shall ride any horse that I wish." She looked at Hedlan. "How much?"

"He's yours. Master Groilin bade me make the bill out to him. I have his tack in the barn. Do you wish to ride him back to the Tavern?" Hedlan shrugged.

Freya was taken aback. *Groilin is paying him. I can't accept a horse like this as a gift; but I also cannot refuse to take him. I'd better talk to Groilin.*

Vrenstalliren took advantage of her surprise.

"Have him gelded first, my Lady. 'T'would be far more suitable a mount then."

Korariettln reared and bared his teeth at the elf.

"If anyone tries to do that to me, I shall rip their throat out!"

Freya laughed at the horse's antics.

"He can come with me as he is. Send his tack over with a groom." She patted the black horse's neck as he regained the ground. "I shall call him Kore though."

She strode to the ring's gate, Kore following at her shoulder. A groom opened the gate and the two left the livery stable's grounds, leaving everyone staring after her.

Chapter Four

"She's a feisty one, Lord." The Jar chuckled. "Mayhap, she would make a better Queen than Mistress."

The Aracan Katuvana shrugged. He moved to the western windows and touched the symbol for the Lych Mistress.

The Jar frowned. "Gmichi! Where are you?"

The ancient Goblin appeared beside the Jar and bowed.

"Don't just stand there, fool. Our Lord needs my voice."

Gmichi picked the Jar up and carried it over to the western windows, depositing it on the pedestal there.

The Aracan Katuvana flicked one finger towards the Goblin who flinched and bowed deeply, before leaving the room.

"You wished my attention, most wonderful of Lords?" The Lych Mistress's sultry tones washed over them, and the Jar grinned at the Aracan's sigh before it spoke.

"How are Lady Erendell and Sir Grald doing in their training, Lady Lych?"

"Erendell has excelled at Dark Mistress Training and would be a good choice for the Higher Caste. Not surprising considering her lineage. Sir Grald will make an excellent Dark Paladin." The Lych Mistress laughed. "He is already surpassing many of the Drow candidates."

"We will need Sir Grald for a mission shortly. Is he ready?" The Jar asked as the Aracan Katuvana selected another symbol and brought up a training room where Grald fought against a Poison Demon.

"He should be. Are we beginning at last, My Lord?" The Lych Mistress clapped her hands in childlike excitement.

"Lady Freya is indeed almost to the designated dungeon, Lady Lych."

"Wonderful! I shall put my minions to work at once." She curtsied deeply and a strangled noise emerged from beneath the Aracan Katuvana's hood as her cleavage was revealed. "Thank you for honouring me so."

"Thank you, Lady Lych." The Jar said as the Aracan Katuvana switched views, bringing Grald into the main view.

The Aracan Katuvana and the Jar watched as Grald severed both of the Poison Demon's horns with one swift pass of his oversized sword, before cleaving the demon in two, green ichor spraying over everything in the vicinity.

"He's not even breaking a sweat, despite that armour," the Jar remarked as Grald flicked the ichor off his blade and turned toward them.

"My Lord Aracan," Grald bowed in greeting. "I hope this morning finds you well."

The Aracan Katuvana nodded.

"Sir Grald. It is time for your departure to Jinra. Your sister is in the next town over," the Jar told him. "Do you remember your orders?"

Grald bowed.

"Yes. I am to bring her in as swiftly as possible so the expansion to the East can begin. I thank my Lord for allowing me into his confidence."

The Jar smiled.

"Lady Lych assures us of your total loyalty. Besides, it would not do for the first Emperor of Elysia to be uninformed of his fate."

"I understand," Grald nodded. "I will not let you down."

"Good." The Jar's eye slid round to look at the Aracan before returning to look at the window again. "Our Lord has a great deal of confidence in you."

The Aracan Katuvana waved one hand and Grald's eyes dilated with pleasure.

"Thank you for your favour, my Lord. May I have leave to see my wife before I depart?"

"Indeed, you may." The Jar watched as the man ran out of the arena. "Have fun, Sir Grald."

The Aracan Katuvana snapped his fingers and the pictures disappeared from the window, leaving him gazing out over the lake surrounding the tower.

"And so it begins, my Lord," the Jar murmured.

KRAARZ AND LIN WATCHED Lady Freya walk away, the black stallion's coat shining like satin under the noon sun as he followed her.

"She certainly has the right attitude, Lin," Kraarz commented as they made their way back to the Tavern through the midday crowds.

"I believe your spirits may be correct, Kraarz," Lin smiled. "I have not seen such regal bearing and temperament in anyone except our late Empress. Lady Freya may indeed be the Heir."

"We should introduce ourselves without delay." Kraarz quickened his step, using his staff to navigate past a knot of traders haggling over a load of grain.

"What if she will not return to Elysia with us?" Lin frowned and a small blonde boy carrying a tray of baked goods skipped out of her way.

"Then we shall accompany her until she will. The Spirits shall send us aid," Kraarz said.

They turned into the stableyard beside the Tavern. Lady Freya stood at the door of a loosebox, feeding the black stallion chunks of carrot and apple.

"Lady Freya, I presume?" Kraarz strode up to her and bowed deeply.

"You must be the Urakh Shaman that Master Groilin said wanted to speak to me." The girl laid one hand on her stallion's neck as his lip curled up. "Steady Kore. Groilin said he was a friend."

The horse snorted and turned away from the Urakh.

Kraarz smiled. "May I introduce my companion to you: Samurai Cha Mai Lin of Elysia."

Lin stepped forward. "I am the Aide de Camp of the Late Empress of Elysia. My companion, Kraarz is a Shaman of the Northern Urakh Tribe."

Freya inclined her head to acknowledge them.

"Why are you here?"

"The Late Empress sent me out to find her Heir many, many months ago," Lin bowed toward Freya. "You have the form and face of an Elysian noble."

"Do I? I think you must have me muddled up with someone else," Freya said and turned to look at the pair. "I have no family; they were all killed when I was a child." She seemed ill at ease.

She's lying. Lin realised and changed what she was about to say.

"Only your parents died. They were travelling on a diplomatic mission from the Empress to the Council of Thirteen in Jira," Lin said.

Kraarz shot a startled look at her, and Lin shook her head imperceptibly. *Now is not the time to tell her about the bad blood between her parents and her grandmother. This half truth will suffice.*

"Why are you talking to me then? Surely you should go back to Elysia and report back to her?" Freya frowned.

"I would have done, except..." Lin paused. *She didn't protest the lie. She knows more about her past than she lets on.*

"Except what?" Freya stroked her horse's neck, absently plaiting a few strands of his mane.

"The Empress died recently. There isn't much contact between the Jinran Council and the Court of Elysia, so I doubt you would have heard about it." Lin sighed. "I need to find the heir before I return."

"Why are you involving me in this?" Freya glanced around. *Where's that damn Paladin when I really need him?*

"I believe you are the one who Lin is seeking," Kraarz said.

"And how do you know that?" Freya raised one elegantly shaped eyebrow.

"My companion spirit told me," Kraarz smiled an expression that made Freya feel mildly anxious. "Vox inhabits the Spirit Realm, between the Summerlands and the Mortal World. As a result, Vox can see what everyone was, is and will be. Vox told me that *you* are the one Lin is seeking."

"My name is Freya of Jira. I am travelling to meet my brother, Sir Grald at the next village." She folded her arms. "I have no idea who you are talking about, but I am an orphan, alone, apart from Grald."

Kraarz frowned, his eyes sparkling red in the darkening afternoon.

"Vox is never wrong."

Lin placed her hand on Kraarz's shoulder.

"Don't worry Kraarz. It may be that she will lead us to the heir, rather than actually being the heir. May we travel with you?"

Kraarz opened his mouth to say something, but Lin shook her head slightly, so he shut it again.

"You are welcome to join me on the journey to Jinra. I have no objection to having new companions." Freya smiled. *At least if they are with me, they are not trailing behind me. That would be creepy.*

"But I have an objection, my Lady." Vrenstalliren's voice echoed off the stone buildings around them.

Freya sighed. *What now?*

Vrenstalliren strode over and stood in front of her.

"As your Guardian, I must protest. We know nothing of these people. They could be slavers from Giranath for all you know."

Freya held back a groan. "I didn't ask you to be my guardian, you appointed yourself." *And he still hasn't explained why he hid my identity when we arrived, or why he's insisting on accompanying me like this.*

The Paladin ignored her. "What exactly do you want?" he demanded of the pair. "An elite Elysian Warrior and an Urakh Shaman is an odd pairing, and I am surprised that Master Groilin allows you to stay here."

The silence was deafening.

Freya closed her eyes. *This is going to get nasty. I can feel it.*

"So can I." Kore nudged the back of her shoulder. *"How about you and I go for a ride together? They should have finished fighting by the time we get back."*

Freya's laughter surprised the others in the yard, and they all looked straight at her. For a moment, she panicked. *What do I do now?*

THE SITUATION IN JIREN had a number of interested parties watching...

From I'Mor Barad, the Aracan Katuvana and the Jar watched eagerly as the Urakh Shaman began to incant.

"Would my Lord like to place a small wager on the outcome of the coming skirmish?" the Jar remarked as the Elysian warrior took up a stronger stance in front of the Elf.

The Aracan Katuvana snapped his fingers and a small pile of gold coins appeared in front of the window. He sorted them into three piles and with a gesture created an image of the people the money was on, sitting them on top of the relevant pile.

The Jar grinned. "Excellent idea, Lord. I shall match that, and we'll see what happens." There was a shimmer and matching piles of gold appeared next to Katuvana's.

The window next to the one they were watching lit up and the Lych Mistress appeared.

"Lord, Sir Grald has set off for his mission." She paused and took in the scene. "Are you wagering on something, my most handsome of Lords?"

"Yes, Lady Lych. The Paladin travelling with Sir Grald's sister has got himself into a spot of bother with an Elite Elysian Warrior and an Urakh Shaman in Jiren," the Jar replied, his eye fixed upon the scene playing out on the main window.

The Lych Mistress did something outside her window, studied it and a smile spread over her red lips. "My, my. I never thought my brother would have the guts to do something like this. Mother would kill him... figuratively speaking, of course; my goody, goody mother never even raised her voice to us."

"That is your brother?" the Jar said as Katuvana turned to look at her.

"Oh yes. Vrenstalliren was a baby when I saw him last, still in First Class. I'll put ten gold on him and double the amount on the others." She snapped her fingers and the piles of gold appeared beside the ones the Aracan Katuvana had placed.

"You would bet against your brother?"

"Aranok was more of a man than he could ever be," the Lych Mistress dismissed the Jar's question. "Besides, he is the enemy now. I am my Lord's most loyal follower."

The Aracan made a pleased whistle and with a wave of his hand, a pair of earrings with large rubies in them, appeared in front of the Lych Mistress.

She gasped, flushed and smiled.

"Thank you, Lord! They are divine. I will await your message on the outcome of our wager with pleasure." Her voice dropped a decibel, and she blew a kiss before her window returned to normal.

"I still think she would make an excellent Mistress or even a Wife for you," the Jar grumbled.

The Aracan Katuvana stared at the Jar and the heat of his gaze from underneath his hood made the Jar quiver on its pedestal.

"Look, Lord. The Paladin is drawing his sword!" the Jar distracted the Aracan Katuvana and breathed a quiet sigh of relief when the gaze was directed at the scene on the window.

Chapter Five

A Blue Banded Hawk perched on the roof of the Golden Dice, her head cocked so that she could watch the fight starting below. Inside her head, a voice was speaking, but she could only understand the emotion of the words and not the content.

"Why is the child just standing there? She needs to stop this. If the next few weeks are to be resolved smoothly, these two need to accompany her, not attack her guardian." Calliale's frustration boiled over and startled the hawk into flapping her wings. *"Sorry, my friend, but I can't help it! Why is it that Father allows Espilieth to interfere in the Human's lives and not me?"*

The hawk settled again and waggled her tail.

Calliale watched as the Paladin and the Elysian feinted and circled. The Urakh Shaman had finished his incantation and now an amorphous sphere of green light floated over his shoulder. *"Why is an Otherworld Spirit involved in this? Is Vaarzasia trying to influence things?"*

The hawk made a soft keeing noise in the back of her throat.

"I know, I know. It's not her fault that one of her Shamans is here, but they are the best two for the job. They might at least be able to get the child out of there alive."

The hawk shifted from one foot to the other as the combatants lashed out at each other. Calliale lost sight of the girl as they moved in front of her. *"Damn. Can you get any closer to her?"* The Hawk shook herself. *"Fair enough. I suppose it would look a bit odd if..."*

A pulse of jubilation made the Hawk flap rapidly in surprise. She called out and Calliale answered. *"I've had an idea..."*

FREYA GAVE UP PLEADING with Vrenstalliren. The elf had ignored her all the way and had drawn his sword on Kraarz when he started incanting, forcing Lin to protect the Shaman. She tried one last time to get through the Paladin's thick skull.

"Vrenstalliren, all he is doing was proving who he is! There's no need of this."

He replied haughtily.

"I'm sorry, my Lady, but I take my responsibilities very seriously. He has committed a hostile action by summoning a possibly evil spirit to..."

Freya rolled her eyes as his visor cut off the rest of his speech. She looked across at Kraarz.

"I'm sorry about this, Kraarz."

"'Tis not your fault, Lady Freya. Let Lin pound some sense into him. She's very good at that, I don't think she'll hurt him a great deal." The Urakh looked up at the emerald green ball of light that appeared above his shoulder. "It's about time you arrived, Vox."

The light pulsed and Freya heard a clear voice from it inside her head, the same way that she heard Kore.

"I was busy. I don't have to hang around you all the time, Kraarz."

Kraarz laughed.

"Lady Freya, may I introduce Vox, my Otherworld Spirit Companion and general ego deflator."

The light floated over to Freya as Lin and Vrenstalliren circled in front of her. Freya could see that Lin wasn't even trying to attack the Paladin, just defending and counterattacking his blows.

"So, you are the next Empress of Elysia. I told Kraarz that you were." The light's smug tone made Freya giggle. *"You're a pretty one as well. It must come from your father's side, your mother, aunt, and grandmother were all as plain as unseasoned Virax."*

"So, you are Vox. I'm pleased to make your acquaintance," Freya replied, smiling.

"Polite too. Your Grandmother let her position go to her head and it made her and your aunt arrogant. That's why your parents were banished after their marriage." Vox floated back to Kraarz. *"She felt your father's rank was too far beneath your mother's."*

"Don't be insolent, Vox. Lady Freya doesn't know much about her parents. They were killed when she was small."

"I know. I talked to them for you, remember?" Vox settled onto the skull on Kraarz's staff. *"They asked me to tell you that they love you and your brother, even though he's gone over to the enemy."*

"What?" Freya's heart lurched. "What do you mean gone over to the enemy?"

"Whoops! I'll talk to you about it later. For the moment, you're going to need to stand up strong and hold still." The light pulsed.

"Wh...Why?"

"Just do it!" Vox snapped.

Freya's self-preservation instincts, finely honed by her life as a pleasure slave swung into action, and she braced herself.

With a scream, a blue-banded hawk swooped out of the sky, grabbed Vrenstalliren's sword out of his hand, dropped it in front of Freya and circled back towards the Elysian.

Lin dropped her blade point and bowed her head.

"I understand, Lady Calliale, I shall not fight my comrades."

The Hawk screeched once and flew back to Freya.

"Hold your arm out." Vox hissed.

Freya raised her right arm and the hawk dropped lightly onto it. The Hawk didn't seem to weigh as much as it looked. *Why isn't my arm torn to shreds by those talons? They have to be a good three inches long.*

Lin's eyes widened and she sheathed her sword hurriedly, before dropping to one knee in front of Freya.

Vrenstalliren stared first at Lin, and then at Freya. His eyes dropped to his sword that lay at Freya's feet. Finally, he looked up at the massive Hawk on her arm. His jaw dropped.

"Lady Calliale has bestowed her favour upon Lady Freya and from this moment on, I serve only her." Lin bowed her head and extended her arms, crossing them at the wrists.

"I have to say that this Calliale person knows how to break a fight up with style," Kore said, shaking his mane.

"Um, thank you Lin. I appreciate this." Freya looked at the Hawk, then at the bouncing bubble of light. "What's going on, Vox?"

"Calliale is the Elven Goddess of Truth. She is bound to act only through her messenger, after she caused the Ten Thousand Clan War in Giranath by upsetting their Chief of Chiefs." Vox laughed and its light flickered in time. *"That's the problem with telling the Truth all the time, sometimes people don't want to hear it."*

The Hawk shrieked and took off again, disappearing into the clouds.

"See. She doesn't like it when it's done to her," Vox pulsed once. *"Kraarz, I'll be back later. Don't let this happen too often, will you?"*

"I shall endeavour to keep control of the situation, Vox." Kraarz bowed his head as Vox winked out.

Vrenstalliren looked confused.

"Fair Maiden. What is going on?"

Freya made a sudden decision.

"Sir Paladin, I have something to tell you and I fear you will not like it."

He frowned, stooped and retrieved his sword, wiping dirt away from the blade with his cloak.

"Do you wish to speak in private?"

"Yes, Sir Paladin, I do."

Lin stood up.

"Kraarz and I shall return to the common room, your highness."

"Thank you, Lin." Freya smiled and took the elf's arm. "Walk with me, Prince Vrenstalliren."

GRALD ARRIVED IN THE Jinra Dungeon as the sun rose. What he found was a shambles.

"Where is your Custodian?" he demanded.

"Well, you see…" the warlock he'd collared on arrival said, "…our Custodian was killed trying to separate the Vampires and the Skeletons. He'd placed their Lairs far too close together and…" the warlock trailed off as he caught sight of Grald's face.

The Dark Paladin resisted the urge to split the Warlock down the middle.

"Do you have a Devil Demon?"

"Goraln? He never comes out of his quarters. When Custodian Theraldin ordered him to intervene in the undead battle, Goraln refused to do his bidding," another warlock said, his arms full of heavy books.

"Has no one thought to tell the Aracan Katuvana of this situation?" Grald snapped.

The two warlocks looked at each other.

"I thought not. Lead me to your Dais Room."

The unencumbered warlock bowed and turned.

"It is this way, Dark Paladin."

Grald looked at the other warlock.

"Put those books back in the library and summon all the creatures to the main hall for a meeting. I will be there shortly."

"Yes, Dark Paladin." The warlock staggered away towards the library.

Well, that went better than expected. Grald thought as he strode along the corridor from the Dais Room. *The Aracan Katuvana seems to be in a good mood today.* He strode through a large Lair, not even noticing the foul stench of the Poison Demons or the thick grey sludge the Giant Slugs left behind. A small pause at the Guard Post to make sure that the Skeletons on duty were paying attention and he was out into the main, encircling passageway.

He paused as a mass of Gremlins rushed past him.

Who are the Gremlins taking food to? Grald followed the stream of gremlins carrying featherless, clucking chickens. It turned out to be the same direction that the Aracan Katuvana had implanted in his mind for the Devil Demon.

This place is a mess, Grald frowned as he noticed the floor was still packed dirt. Swinging one arm out, he grabbed a Gremlin and hoisted it into the air in front of him.

"Why has this corridor not been paved and fortified?"

"Feed... feed," the pathetic creature gibbered. "Must...feed."

"Feed what?"

"Feed... Horny." The Gremlin wriggled; sweat rolling down its scaly face. Grald let it go with a casual slap to the head.

The gremlin bowed deeply.

"Thank you!" it cried before it scrambled away at top speed.

Grald followed, his temper deteriorating as he took in the complete disarray of the walls.

"No fortifications, no traps, not even any torches." He passed the corridor marked as leading to the Prison, which didn't even have a door and passed through a propped open, thick oak door with rusting hinges and lock.

Swinging the barely adequate inner door open, Grald strode into the lair of this dungeon's devil demon. "Goraln!"

A bulging red mass sprawled on a dirty mattress looked in his direction. Only the horns identified its head as being that of a Devil Demon.

"That is my name. Who calls me by it?"

Grald licked his lips with distaste.

"Your Aracan does. Do you still serve him?"

"Human, I serve no one, but myself. Go away." The corpulent demon growled and grabbed a gremlin. "Get Theraldin immediately." He dropped it to the floor again.

The Gremlin spun in a circle, confused by the request to fetch someone who didn't exist. Grald bit his lip in amusement.

"You dare laugh at Goraln?" the devil demon hauled himself to his feet, scattering bones over the gremlins. The tiny creatures gathered them up and fled the room.

"So, you *can* move." Grald loosened his sword in its sheath. "You have been delinquent in your duties. The Aracan Katuvana has sent me on a mission of importance and the Dungeon is in disarray."

"It is Theraldin's duty to look after the dungeon, not mine."

"When the Custodian is killed, the next highest in rank takes over until another custodian can be named," Grald said.

"You dare quote the Overlaws to me? I, who was there at the start?" Goraln roared and lunged at him.

Grald waited until the demon had committed himself to the move and smoothly stepped out of the way. Goraln stumbled over the still spinning gremlin and fell with a blubbery splat onto the unscrubbed flagstones, crushing the gremlin to pulp. Drawing his blade, Grald held the point to the Devil Demon's neck, piercing the skin enough to allow blood to trickle down his ruddy skin and pool in front of Goraln's nose, mixing with the gremlin's ichor.

"I am the Custodian of this Dungeon now and I have orders for you." Grald twisted the point and Goraln flailed. "We are expecting guests, and you will get your fat, flabby butt into the Training Room to be in the right condition to deal with them."

"I won't be able to get into shape that fast!" the demon protested.

Grald's eyes narrowed, and a gold covering slid across them. He slapped the Demon hard across the head with his free hand, driving the blade into his neck with the effort. Then, as the Demon gurgled and thrashed on the floor, he removed the sword and healed Goraln, then lifted him up, using one horn as a handle. "Get into the Training Room and you will find the flab will melt away if you work hard enough."

"Yes, Lord!" Goraln recognised the Aracan Katuvana's possession of the human. When he was dropped, he scrambled to his knees, bowed, and then scurried off to his training faster than a gremlin on a pay break.

The possession disappeared and Grald grinned.

"Now to deal with the rest of them." He wiped his sword and exited the complex, heading for the main hall.

Chapter Six

The Northern Woods loom on the horizon, a great bear of ancient trees surrounding the honey pot of Jinra Village. Freya laughed at her own whimsy and endured the irritated glare from Vrenstalliren in front of her.

"Methinks your Guardian Paladin is a little annoyed with you," Kraarz said as he walked beside her horse.

"He thinks I'm innocent and naïve. He also thinks I'm being taken for a ride by Giranathian Slavers," she sighed. "He refused to believe the truth when I told it to him."

"That you're a manumitted Pleasure Slave who might be the Empress of Elysia?" Kraarz grinned up at her. "Even though I know it's true, it does sound straight out of a fairytale."

"Elves are arrogant like that, no matter where they're from," Lin commented from behind her.

Vrenstalliren snorted and kneed Ohtár on into a gallop.

"Don't go too far!" Freya called.

The elf raised a hand in acknowledgement and carried on up the long hill.

"*Why does that dumb stallion get to run and I don't?*" Kore complained.

Freya soothed him by stroking his mane.

"I don't want to tire you out. You were in that livery stable a long time."

"You just don't want to leave Kraarz behind," Lin said, moving up beside her. She rode Vrenstalliren's mare, and the packhorse had been left behind at the Golden Dice until he returned to collect it.

Freya shrugged, admitting the point.

"He's walking, we're riding."

"There hasn't been a horse born that can outpace me," Kraarz said, speeding up.

How does he see where he's going? He's blind. Freya still hadn't got used to the Urakh and his white eyes made her shudder whenever she saw them.

Unbidden, Kore matched pace with the Urakh. Lin exchanged a smiled with Freya as the white mare quickened her pace to keep up with the stallion.

"No horse can outpace him, huh? Well, we'll see about that," Kore said.

It was the only warning that Freya had. The stallion broke into a canter, his long legs eating up the distance.

Kraarz kept up with the horse. The mare quickly fell behind with Lin. Kore broke into a gallop and Kraarz had to run to keep up.

Freya giggled as they shot past Vrenstalliren. The Paladin's jaw dropped open and he booted Ohtár into a gallop behind them.

"SIR GRALD, YOUR EFFORTS in the Jinra dungeon are commendable. I have never seen it look so...so..." The Jar stuttered to a halt speechless for once.

The Aracan Katuvana clapped his hands and a large leather bag appeared in front of Grald, who opened it.

"Thank you, My Lord. I merely do my duty in your service." Grald ran a handful of emeralds through his fingers, his eyes shining with reflected light from the gems. "With your permission, I shall continue to make the place presentable for our visitors."

The Aracan Katuvana nodded and Grald's picture cleared.

"Who would have known the Barbarian had it in him to get Goraln back into shape that fast. He will make a wonderful Emperor," the Jar said.

The Aracan Katuvana shrugged and turned back to the Crystal Ball beside the throne that showed Lady Freya's progress.

"What will you do with his sister, Lord?" the Jar asked. "It looks like she may be about to get side tracked."

They watched as Freya, the Urakh and Vrenstalliren raced across the rolling hills of north-western Jinran. They didn't seem to care where they went.

"They're going in the right direction, but if they stray too far from the road, they'll miss the village and get lost in the woods." The Jar groaned in frustration. "Why can't you humans do as you're told?"

The Aracan Katuvana growled.

"I wasn't talking about you, Lord," the Jar said quickly.

Ignoring the Jar, the Aracan Katuvana appeared to be thinking. He gestured and a black book floated over to him from a shelf. Thumbing through it, the Aracan Katuvana was clearly considering his options.

"Is that the Big Black Book of Bad Beasts, Lord?" The Goblin brought the Jar back to the pedestal beside the throne as the Aracan Katuvana sat down.

The Aracan Katuvana stopped flipping through the pages and a pleased sound emerged from the hood. He showed the page to the Jar, who smiled.

"Ah yes. I shall contact Lord Jarsken without delay." The goblin picked the Jar up again and carried it out of the room.

The Aracan Katuvana tossed the massive book over his shoulder and went back to watching Freya race the Urakh Shaman.

THE SHADOW APPEARED from behind a cloud and flowed across the waving sea of grass carpeting Jinran. Small at first, as it reached Jira it grew rapidly and caused a few startled birds to fly for the nearest tree.

"WHAT IN ESPILIETH'S Holy Name are you two doing?" Vrenstalliren demanded when he finally caught up with Kraarz and Freya.

Freya laughed and dismounted from Kore, moving around to face the big black stallion. "It wasn't my idea, Vren. Kore challenged Kraarz to keep up with him and he did."

"Don't call me Vren. Only my sisters call me that." Vrenstalliren waved the explanation aside. "I knew it was a bad idea for a maiden to ride a stallion. They just can't control them."

Kore snorted, blowing wisps of Freya's dark hair out of their plait. *"That elf needs a lesson in good manners. Talking about me as if I was a mere beast like his dumb animal."*

"Steady, Kore." Freya soothed the irritated creature. "He didn't mean it as an insult to you, just as an insult to my riding skills."

Vrenstalliren blanched.

"I would never..."

"He turns an interesting shade of pale, don't you think?" Lin said to Kraarz as she arrived.

The Urakh snorted and shook his head.

"I'm staying out of this."

PASSING OVER JIREN, the shadow's size made many villagers glance up and then hurry for shelter in the nearest building.

A herd of sheep stampeded for a copse of trees on the eastern bank of the river Ranin as the shadow enlarged over them, their panicking shepherd and his dogs trying desperately to stop them from plunging into the river.

THE SCENT OF SULPHUR carried by a rapidly strengthening wind made Kraarz wrinkle his nose.

"We have to get out of here, find shelter."

"Why? It's a lovely sunny day, Jinra isn't all that far away and we haven't had lunch yet." Freya looked at him. "What's the matter?"

Lin looked concerned.

"Have you had a message?"

Kraarz shook his head.

"Not from Vox. Just one of my own hunches." He started in the direction of the trees.

Ohtár and the Mare shrieked as a strong sulphur smell washed over the group. Lin, still mounted, controlled the mare with consummate ease, but Vrenstalliren had the reins wrenched out of his hand as the Charger reared.

The Paladin grabbed Ohtár's bridle as he came back down and fought to calm him.

"Get on my back. I have to run, or we will not survive." Kore started moving in the same direction as Kraarz.

Freya grabbed his bridle and managed to stop him while she mounted. *"Why?"*

"What's going on?" Vrenstalliren sounded confused, but he followed Freya's lead.

"I don't know, but Kraarz is never wrong, and something has spooked the animals, so I suggest we follow suit!" Lin told him.

"There's a dragon heading towards us. Kraarz was right, we have to get to the trees." Kore said as he put his head down and galloped.

Lin and Vrenstalliren followed, the Paladin still shouting, "Why are we running?"

He started to draw rein, his face angry, but as the charger slowed, an ear-shattering roar from behind him set the horse running again.

Freya glanced back.

"Dragon!" she shouted to Vrenstalliren. "Come on."

As they drew level with Kraarz, Lin leaned down and scooped him up onto the mare, and then all of them clung to their mounts as they ran for the woods.

Kore began to veer north. *"The trees are closer there."*

A fireball shot past Freya and impacted to her right, setting the grass aflame, scaring Ohtár and the mare.

Kore let out a strange sound, half neigh, half scream. *"That should have hit us. Dragons rarely miss their targets."* He shifted his path to avoid the flames and sped up, still heading north.

Another fireball hit the ground just ahead of them and the whumph as the flames spread made Freya shriek. Kore turned left rapidly, his hooves carving chunks of sod from the ground.

"There's something odd about this attack," Lin called over as the white mare drew closer. "Dragons don't normally miss, especially from this close. It's like we're being herded."

Vrenstalliren shook his head.

"How many dragons have you fought, Elysian? We have to get to the trees and the closest ones are to the north." He turned Ohtár's head north and clapped his heels to the stallion's flanks. Ohtár charged, gathered himself and leapt over the flames.

"Fool." Kraarz snorted. "This delicate mare would never make that jump."

Freya agreed and they continued heading Northwest.

The dragon veered north and after a short while, they slipped into the trees, the horses' hooves crunching on the fallen leaves.

"I do believe the monster has followed Sir Vrenstalliren," Kraarz said, dropping down from the back of the white mare and walking alongside.

"We're not far from the road here," Lin said after a few moments of consulting her map.

"We'll carry on into Jinra then. I'm sure Vrenstalliren can look after himself," Freya said. *I know I didn't ask him to be my protector, but I hope he can get away from the dragon.* She looked back into the woods as they rode away.

"I SWEAR THAT POTHOLE was three feet deep," Kraarz complained, pulling at his soaked clothing. Red mud streaks turned his already strange face into something out of a Valdierian epic.

"This isn't a well-travelled road," Freya shrugged. "I doubt the locals even try and keep it maintained."

"I can see that," the Urakh grumbled.

The trees lining the sides of the road gave way onto a large clearing in the Northern Woods. In front of them a palisade rose, smooth sharpened logs stabbing up at the overcast sky.

"The gate's closed." Lin frowned. "This is a village, isn't it?"

"According to my brother's note. He said he'd meet me here, at the Cuddly Cub Inn."

Lin looked up at the palisade and the gate.

"Well, they've been busy, fairly recently I'd say; these fortifications are new."

"Ho, the Village!" Kraarz called out. "Three travellers require a hostelry to clean up and rest while we await the rest of our party."

A hatch opened to one side of the gate and a guard peered out.

"You ain't got no monsters wid ya have..." there was a gasp and the hatch slid shut again.

Freya sighed and moved up to where the hatch had appeared. Dismounting, she knocked on it.

The hatch slid aside a little and an eye appeared in the gap.

"We ain't lettin' ya in. Not wid that...thing."

Freya slipped her hand into the gap and stopped the guard from closing it again.

"He's not a thing. He's my Doctor and Lin is my Trainer. I vouch for them both." She heard whispers coming from the other side as the guard looked away. "Please let us in. We need to rest and eat."

"Who are you?"

Freya smiled.

"I am Freya of Jira, Head Dancer from the Hall of The Black Swan."

Another gasp. More whispers, only this time, they ended with one gate being opened cautiously. Two guards stepped out; their halberds pointed at Kraarz. A third man in a red robe and gold chain stood behind them.

"We were told to expect you, Lady Freya, but not with these two strangers. Sir Grald said you were travelling with an Elven Paladin." The third man said.

"My brother is here?" Freya caught her breath.

"No, my Lady. He went on a mission for the village. We shall allow your companions to enter the fortifications, as you have vouched for them." The red robed man bowed "Be welcome to Jinra. I am Mayor Headstoner."

Chapter Seven

"Everyone is almost in place, Lord," the Jar said as they watched the elven Paladin elude the dragon and head back towards the road. "Would you like to contact Sir Grald?"

The Aracan Katuvana shook his head and moved a piece on his game board.

"Hmm. An interesting manoeuvre. I shall set it in motion at once." The goblin carried the Jar into the next room.

The Aracan Katuvana listened to the shouting and cursing that filled the air for several moments before snapping his fingers. The heavy oak door shut with a crash, dulling the noise. He moved back to the window showing the Paladin reach the palisade around Jinra.

As the Aracan Katuvana watched, a horde of dragon spawn swarmed out of the surrounding woods, overpowered the Paladin and was about to carry him away when Sir Grald rode into the horde's midst.

"SO, HE FREED ME, AND we defeated the Dragon Spawn together," Vrenstalliren boasted, downing his tenth cup of Copperberry wine. "Must have been nearly two hundred of them. I accounted for at least half of the bodies."

"There were seventy and he killed twenty," Grald murmured to Freya.

She giggled and laid her head against his shoulder, sighing happily.

"I'm glad you're here, brother. I was worried about you."

"When have I ever let you down, Lil Sis?" Grald slipped his arm around her and kissed her forehead. "I'll always be with you from now on."

Vrenstalliren poured another cup of wine and toasted Grald with it.

"Here's to Sir Grald, a veritable powerhouse of a knight, with the loveliest sister in existence."

The whole common room cheered and cries of "Sir Grald!"; "Sir Grald the Brave!"; "Sir Grald and Lady Freya of Jira!"; "To the Lovely Lady Freya!" rang off the rafters.

Freya blushed rosily.

Grald grinned at his sister's expression.

"Thank you, Prince Vrenstalliren. Both for your compliments and the care you have taken of my sister on her journey north from Jira."

"'Twas nothing, Sir Grald. She is a wonderful travelling companion." Vrenstalliren burped, coloured and looked surprised as he slid off his seat.

Freya laughed. "Maybe you ought to take him up to his room, Grald."

"Probably a good idea," he said and then lowered his tone. "Will you be okay with these two?" He flicked one finger at Lin and Kraarz, who sat on the opposite side of the table.

"Of course I will. Besides, they saved my life," Freya frowned at her brother. "That dragon would have had me for lunch without them."

He shrugged and got up, retrieved a lightly snoring Vrenstalliren from the floor under the table, slung him over his shoulder and carried the elf up the Cuddly Cub's stairs.

With the two heroes out of the room, the common room settled down again. Freya sipped her mug of mulled wine and looked at Kraarz.

"Is Vrenstalliren's story true?" she asked, her voice loud enough to carry to the Urakh's sensitive ears.

"I was wondering that too, your Highness," Lin said.

"I shall find out, My Lady." Kraarz closed his eyes and began to hum a strangely compelling melody. Lin watched the crowd around them with wary eyes, one hand on her long knife.

Kraarz opened his eyes and Freya held in a gasp. His eyes were emerald green from edge to edge.

"A Horde of Dragon Spawn attacked the Paladin as he alleged," Kraarz said, but it wasn't the Urakh's voice.

"Vox?" Freya whispered.

"In Kraarz' flesh, indeed it is me. You are even more beautiful in the physical realm than your soul is in the Otherworld." Vox/Kraarz winked.

Freya was speechless.

"So, the Paladin is telling the truth. Excellent. What of Sir Grald?" Lin asked. "Did he really just arrive at the right moment?"

"That is the truth, Lin, but all else is lies. He has made a pact with the Dark Gods." Vox/Kraarz told her. "Freya, you must leave here immediately."

I can't believe that. My brother is good! Freya shook her head.

"I will not leave my brother's side.

"I shall remain with you then. You are far more important than you realise, or Calliale would not be trying to protect you," Vox/Kraarz said. "Look for my arrival tomorrow morning."

Kraarz closed his eyes again and when he opened them, it was to reveal his normal white ones. "What did my friend say?"

Lin quickly related the conversation.

"I see." He sighed. "I do hate it when Vox does this. He always manages to hinder more than he helps."

"Well, I'm going to have a bath and go to bed." Freya stood up.

Lin stood quickly. "I have sworn to serve you and serve you I shall. A bath sounds like a wonderful idea."

Kraarz laughed.

"If you two are going to retire, then I will also. I fear that without your positive presence in the room, I may be in danger."

The three of them headed for the stairs.

Grald was in the process of coming down.

"Going to bed already, Freya? I was hoping to catch up with you. I have lots of news."

"I'm tired and I need a bath. Lin and I are sharing a room, so I will be perfectly safe with her." Freya smiled, stood on her tiptoes and kissed Grald's cheek. "I will see you in the morning. Good night, Graldai."

"YOU HUMANS TAKE FOREVER to wake up." A small voice by Freya's ear shocked her into wakefulness.

She turned her head to find a small, silver-furred Flixen cub with emerald green eyes curled on the pillow beside her. "Vox?"

"How many Flixen do you know that talk?" the cub licked her cheek with its pale pink tongue. "It's four hours after dawn."

Freya yawned, covering her mouth with her hand. *If it weren't for those tiny little wings, Vox might get mistaken for a kitten. O'course, Flixen aren't exactly well-known animals outside of Elysia, but I'm not sure where I've seen them either.* The gap in her memory made her frown as she sat up.

"Time for breakfast then." She pushed back the covers and swung her feet around. Lin wasn't in the room, but her bed had been made. "Lin must be downstairs."

The Flixen watched while she washed.

"You have a definite resemblance to your father and your mother's shape is far more appealing on you than it was on her of course, you are as tall as your great grandfather."

Freya ignored the comments. "Do you want me to call you by name?"

"You might as well. Lin and Kraarz will know who I am, but your brother and that blind Paladin who insists on protecting you, won't." Vox stood up and stretched like a cat. "By the way, Kore is feeling rather lonely. How about we go for a ride this morning?"

Freya smiled.

"I can't see why not. After all I have two heroes, an Urakh Shaman and an elite Elysian warrior to protect me." She pulled out one of the riding dresses she'd bought in Jiren and slipped into it, smoothing the tight bodice over her toned abdomen. "Would you like me to carry you?"

Vox turned a somersault.

"That would be wonderful. This creature form may have wings, but until the body matures, I can't fly."

Freya finished dressing quickly and swung a thick woollen cloak around her shoulders before she held her hands out. The fox-eared animal jumped into them and scrambled up her arm, the tiny cat-claws gripping the thick woollen material until it reached Freya's shoulder.

"Thank you," Vox purred into Freya's ear, swiping its bushy tail up under her long plait around her neck like a scarf.

The dancer smiled and left the room.

The common room was half-empty. Lin and Kraarz sat at the same table they had occupied last night. Grald and Vrenstalliren were nowhere to be seen.

"Good morrow, Lady Freya. Vox informed me that you were awake and what to order for you to break your fast." The Urakh smiled.

Freya was mildly surprised to find that she no longer thought of Kraarz as strange looking. "Thank you, Kraarz."

"Your brother and the Paladin have gone out to inspect Kore. I think Vrenstalliren is still trying to get you what he calls *a more suitable mount for a maiden*." Lin told her, looking mildly amused.

Freya laughed.

"I suspect that Kore will have something to say about that." She sat beside Lin and thanked the barmaid who brought her porridge over.

A comfortable silence settled over the table as they ate. Even Vox seemed disinclined to say anything.

"Freya!" Grald burst into the room.

She looked up.

"What's wrong?"

"Your stallion has gone crazy! I'm going to get the local Farrier to put it down," her brother said.

Freya rolled her eyes and looked at Vox who had curled up in her lap.

"Vrenstalliren is trying to ride Kore. Kore is trying to unseat him." The Flixen purred.

"Don't tell me. Vrenstalliren is insisting that Kore is an unsuitable mount for a delicate maiden such as myself and decided to try and ride Kore to prove his point." Freya sighed. "Don't bother with the Farrier. I'll deal with this."

"Freya, the animal is frothing at the mouth. It's mad!" Grald tried to block her as she picked up Vox and made for the stableyard door.

"That horse is as intelligent as you or me, Sir Grald," Kraarz said. "The Lady has proved on more than one occasion that she can control him."

"I didn't ask for your opinion, *Urakhiiz*," Grald snapped.

Lin's hand dropped to her sword hilt, but Kraarz shook his head at her and shrugged.

"Urakhiiz? I haven't heard that one since I was an Urakhling," he laughed.

"Come on, Grald. Let me show you what I can do, before you decide to have *my horse* put down." Freya pushed her brother aside and strode out.

In the stable yard, the Inn's grooms and stableboys had gathered to watch the show.

In the centre, Kore was on his hind legs and Vrenstalliren held on grimly.

"I'll tame you, beast," the elf prince snarled.

"You'll do no such thing," Freya called out, noticing that the Paladin had spurs on and there was blood on the points. Her eyes narrowed. "Get off my friend."

Kore dropped to the ground, sparks flying out from beneath his hooves.

"I'm glad you're here. Can I get rid of this pest please?"

"Yes, you can. Just make sure he lands somewhere soft," Freya replied.

Kore tossed his head.

"I have just the place."

The black stallion spun, his mane, tail and feathers flying out. Vrenstalliren gasped and tried to keep his seat, but as he slipped sideways, Kore bucked sharply and the elf lost his grip on the reins.

Vrenstalliren sailed through the air. He landed face down in the Inn's manure pile.

The watching crowd burst out laughing and cheered as Kore settled and trotted over to Freya. He nuzzled her hair.

She examined his flanks.

"At least these are just scratches."

"I have a wonderful ointment that will soothe them," Kraarz said. "And if I use a small incantation, he will be as good as new in a few moments."

Freya stroked Kore's nose. *"Will you let him?"*

"Yes. Just don't let those two brutes near me again." Kore neighed and bared his teeth at Grald who took a step back.

"Go with Kraarz and Lin please, Kore," Freya said aloud.

Lin took Kore's reins and the three of them went back into the stables.

Freya waited until the crowd had dispersed and then she rounded on her brother.

"I am not four anymore, Grald. Since you left, I have had to protect myself and I can do without all this male intervention."

"Vrenstalliren wanted me to approve your horse. I didn't touch him!" Grald held his hands up palm out.

"That's not the point."

"Hah. It was him who suggested the spurs," Vox said, *"And gave him the ones he is wearing."*

Freya looked at the paladin who had been helped up by a pair of Stable hands, and was cleaning his hands and face with water from the pump. The wheel spurs he wore had longer points than normal and as the water splashed down over Vrenstalliren's boots, it spun them. There was sparkle and she realised that they'd been sharpened.

She shuddered. "Sharpened spurs, Grald? It was always you had to use spurs to control horses when we were children. Not me." *But then again, I had barely started riding when they died. I just remember father telling Grald off for sharpening his spurs."*

Grald said nothing.

"Now, as soon as Kraarz has finished healing my friend, I am going out riding in the woods. You can come along too; if you think you can keep up." Freya left him and headed for the stables.

Grald's jaw dropped open for a few seconds, and then he snapped it shut. *Who knew you had such a strong will?* He smiled and a thin ribbon of gold surrounded his pupils. *However, little sister, you have given me the perfect opportunity to advance my Lord's plans.* He turned and went into the inn.

Chapter Eight

"Well now, Lord," the Jar said with a pleased smile. "It seems that Sir Grald has managed his mission so far with aplomb."

The Aracan Katuvana nodded, watching the girl, Elysian, Urakh and freshly bathed elven Paladin ride out of the village palisade. Another window showed Sir Grald as he rode out of a secret gate at the back of the village.

"Do you wish to add anything to the mix? A little surprise for our Emperor's sister?"

The Aracan Katuvana considered the suggestion, head on fist and hood turned toward the girl's window. Then he shook his head.

"Very well, Lord. This promises to be an interesting ride anyway." The Jar turned its gaze back to the windows.

THE SUNLIGHT FILTERING through the multiple autumn hues of the leaves above dappled Lin's white mare with golds and reds. The birds sang of winter and berries as the group passed along the track, heading towards a small waterfall that the mayor had told Freya about before they set out.

"This is dangerous, Lady Freya," Vrenstalliren said sullenly.

She ignored him, stroking Vox who had draped itself on Kore's neck. *The air around here is so fresh and clean. So different to Jira's dirty streets.*

"I see no threat," she said at last.

"So, the horde of dragon spawn that attacked me yesterday isn't a threat?" Vrenstalliren moved up beside Freya. "There has to be a nest around here to have so many attack that fast."

Freya looked at him and batted her eyelashes. "I have you to protect me."

He groaned and urged his horse ahead of Kore.

"Can I bite him?" Kore asked, lunging slightly as Vrenstalliren's leg passed his head.

Freya held him back. *"Don't you dare!"*

Kore snorted.

Kraarz exchanged a look with Lin, who had dropped back to ride beside Freya, allowing Vrenstalliren to take point.

"You do understand, don't you Lady? These woods are supposed to hold a Dungeon of Doom." Kraarz said.

Freya blinked, "Really? I thought they'd all been cleansed."

Vox coughed and sighed, *"You're so innocent."*

"What's that?" Lin asked.

"You know about The Black Tower War, don't you?" Kraarz sounded surprised.

Freya looked at Lin. "I know it didn't reach beyond Jinran, but that was because the Empire protected the border."

"Oh yes, we are taught about that in school. Sadly, none of my teachers mentioned anything about Dungeons of Doom," Lin shrugged.

"They were the Aracan Katuvana's strongholds and staging points for his invasion. I believe the furthest east the Aracan Katuvana achieved was Jisira." Kraarz looked around. "There was supposed to be one around here that had been created as part of the Aracan Katuvana's northward thrust."

"Why don't we go look for it?" Freya asked. *It's bound to be more exciting than a normal ride.*

"Freya, that's a bad idea. Not all the dungeons were cleansed. Some just had their Custodians destroyed," Vox said aloud, patting Freya's hand with its paw.

"Shush. What happens if Vrenstalliren hears you?" Freya tapped Vox's nose gently with one finger.

"He can't. He's in a cave." Vox pointed with one paw. "Behind the waterfall over there."

"Can you sense a dungeon around here, Vox?" Kraarz asked.

"The Dark Gods shield them from the likes of me. Only a true Deity would be able to tell you."

"Look, let's just go find out why Vrenstalliren is in this cave. He decided to protect me and shouldn't be exploring." Freya nudged Kore in the direction that Vox had indicated.

The cave began to one side of the waterfall. The falls themselves were just as pretty as the mayor had said, so Freya and Lin left their horses with Ohtár who cropped the grass under a large oak tree.

"He doesn't look after his animals properly," Freya murmured, taking the war stallion's saddle off and spreading Ohtár's blanket out over his back. Ohtár snorted and tossed his head.

"I thought you were scared of him," Kore snorted.

"I was at one point. Then I met you." Freya finished by stroking Ohtár's nose. "He's tame compared to you."

"He says thank you," Kore told her as she made him comfortable.

Lin did the same for the mare, "I hope they'll be safe here."

"I'll look after them," Kore told Freya. *"Just hurry up and come back, would you? I don't like this place."* He stamped and snorted.

"Kore is right. There is a peculiar taint in the air, and I can see a strange aura around the cave mouth." Vox jumped to her shoulder, its green eyes glowing slightly. "We need to hurry."

Lin and Kraarz moved in front of Freya as they entered the cave. The ground was damp and in places where moss had grown, the footing slippery and difficult.

"Vrenstalliren! Where are you?" Freya called out and her voice echoed. Of the Paladin, there was no sign.

"This isn't a cave, it's a tunnel mouth," Kraarz murmured. "The echoes are too distorted to be just a cave."

They walked further in. As soon as they got away from the entrance cave, the floor became dry sand and muffled the sound of their footfalls. There was a pale light emanating from the walls.

"Where is that coming from?" Lin reached up and ran her hand along the wall. It came away dusty and when Kraarz looked at Lin's hand he frowned.

"That's the scales of the Cloud Moth. They often inhabit deep caverns in the mountains and they're poisonous. You'd best wash your hand."

Lin rinsed the scales away with some of her water, "Thank you. I had a friend who died of Cloud Moth venom. It's not a pretty death."

"What death is?" Freya murmured.

"You have a point," Kraarz said.

Lin shrugged. "I'd prefer a quick and painless stab to a lingering death while your insides liquefy, any day."

Freya was speechless. *But they're so pretty.* She flinched as one fluttered toward her. Vox snapped at it and the large pale winged creature drifted away, "Thank you Vox."

"Vren! Vrenstalliren!" Freya called again as they kept moving. They'd been walking down the tunnel for nearly an hour. "Where is he?"

She stopped as the others halted in front of her. Lin had her hand on her sword and Kraarz had conjured a ball of light to the head of his staff.

"The flooring in front of me is paved," Lin said. "I am beginning to think this may be that dungeon you were talking about."

Vox dropped down to the ground.

"I'll scout ahead. Where there are Dark influences, there are usually traps." Its paws made no sound, even on the paving.

The rest of them waited on the sand.

Vox snorted.

"Typical of the Dark Gods really, they never change their ways, even when they are defeated time and again." Its voice echoed with derision.

"This happened before?" Freya watched the Flixen sniff around the first few slabs. *Is Vox bigger?*

"When the world was new and the inhabitants young," Kraarz began, "the Gods walked openly upon the surface of Quargard. The Dark Gods gathered all those creatures who were inclined to them and made war upon the Gods of Light."

"Needless to say, they were eventually defeated and imprisoned," Vox interrupted. "We don't have time to go through all that, Kraarz. The Paladin is somewhere down the end of this corridor and there are traps to be disarmed. I can deal with the magic ones, but Lin will have to disarm the physical ones." The Flixen jumped up onto Lin's shoulder and she grunted under its weight.

"You've been overeating, Vox," she grumbled. "You're heavy."

"Never mind that. We have to get moving!" Vox snapped in her ear.

Freya looked at Vox. The Flixen had grown and was now the size of one of the cats Jetara had. *How fast do real Flixen mature?*

Moving onto the paving, Lin and Vox began to disarm traps. Freya and Kraarz followed cautiously behind. Some of the traps were simple pitfalls and spikes, others more elaborate with more than one swinging blade. At one point, they had to run down a side passage to escape a massive boulder that had been released by a careless footfall on Lin's part.

The group stopped, Kraarz gasping for breath as Vox checked the area for traps.

"We're all clear, although I have no idea where we are now." The Flixen pattered off into the darkness.

Kraarz swallowed half his water bottle's contents.

"See why I said Vox causes trouble when it takes physical form?"

Freya shrugged, "It's helped so far."

"Believe me, its just getting started." Kraarz grumbled.

Lin stretched, "This place is like one of the Imperial Labyrinths the Late Empress had built."

"Maybe she was influenced by the Dark Tower?" Freya raised one eyebrow.

"No, by that time your grandmother had lost any sense of propriety," Lin winced. "The labyrinths were built as death sentences for upper class criminals."

They lapsed into silence, Freya beginning to wonder if her family was as good as her mother had always told her.

"I'm beginning to think that there is something else working here," Vox said as it reappeared. "There are no traps at all down here and the corridor ends with a plain door, no Magic or traps. Not even an alarm on the door."

"Are you saying the Dungeon is still inhabited?" Freya asked. "All the stories I've heard, say the creatures in them were made of evil magic and it dispersed when the Aracan Katuvana was defeated."

"Don't be naïve, Freya." Vox wandered over and rubbed up against her legs. "The creatures are as mortal as you. They were created in the same way and live in the same way. It's how they are raised and managed that makes them Evil."

"Too true," Kraarz said sadly. "The Urakh were a part of that evil for thousands of years before The Black Tower War. It is only since we were freed of the Aracan Katuvana that we have become peaceable."

"So, what do we do now?" Freya looked worried. "We have to find Vrenstalliren."

"Why?" Lin raised an eyebrow. "He's insulted you, hurt one of your companions and steadfastly refused to even contemplate that you are intelligent enough to know what you are doing."

"He's the first man to treat me like a human being and not an object to be admired or played with," she replied. "He has protected me at the cost of his own life and delayed his own journey home to do so."

"Then he is honourable and deserving of our help," Kraarz said, from where he had sat down. He hauled himself up, using his staff as a lever. "We shall take the inhabitants of this dungeon at their invitation and enter through the unguarded door."

Vox purred in agreement.

"Lin, you and I shall go first; to make sure there is no danger. Kraarz, can I count on you to shield Freya if there is trouble?"

"Yes, Vox. I shall indeed do as you request." Kraarz pulled out a green cord with a ceramic spiral pendant. "Wear this, my lady and Magic shall bounce away from you."

She took the pendant and slipped its cord over her head.

"Thank you, Kraarz." Taking a deep breath, she smiled at Lin. "Shall we move on then?"

THE JAR WATCHED THE party's progress with a smile on its black stone face. Behind it, the Aracan Katuvana snored on his throne and Gmichi lay beside it, bubbles of saliva popping on his lips before the drool dribbled down to stain his tabard.

I do believe it is time to put the first part of my plan into action, the Jar mused, its eye turning to look at the console beside it. With a whisper of power, the Jar activated the window beside the one showing the Jinra Dungeon. The Lych Mistress's beautiful face appeared, relaxed in sleep. A Hellpuppy curled in the rich red wool cloth that covered the elven woman's striking form. With a second wisp of power, the Jar activated the mindspeech tool, allowing it to reach into the dreams of the Lych Mistress. *"Hear me, Lady Lych. Hear the voice of your Master."*

The woman on the red covered bed stirred slightly and a smile slid across her lips. *"I hear you, my most beloved Lord."* Her mind tone was soft and sleepy.

"Freya has been drawn into the Jinra Dungeon. Sir Grald will soon require the services of his wife to persuade his sister to join us. Make sure that Lady Erendell is ready for the task." The Jar paused and the Lych Mistress nodded in her sleep. *"I will need your presence in I'Mor Barad soon. Prepare yourself to become my bride at last."*

The Jar withdrew from the mind of the Lych Mistress and watched as she gasped, and her eyes opened. Then it shut that window down and went back to watching Freya as she arrived at the door to the main Dungeon.

THE PASSAGEWAY ON THE other side of the door flickered brightly with candles. Freya examined one of the candelabra, a perfect bronze reproduction of a bull's head and jumped back as it opened its eyes, looked at her and the rest of the party, snorted and went back to sleep.

"Minotaur heads," Kraarz said. "One of the few creatures that turned from the dominion of the Dark Gods and were wiped out in retaliation."

"They're still alive," Freya shuddered.

"They can't die," Vox told her. "Like me, the Minotaurs were part magic. But because I am here, they won't alert whoever is in charge of the Dungeon."

"Why?" Lin asked as they walked up the corridor, her eyes darting along the flagstones, searching for trap triggers.

"I have a standing agreement with the Minotaur spirits." The Flixen shrugged, its now hound size shoulders. "We go back a long way."

"Oh." Lin frowned at a large lump on the floor in front of her. "Is this a magic trap, Vox?"

Vox padded forward and sniffed the lump carefully.

"No. It's physical."

Lin knelt down and began to disarm the trap with Vox's whispered comments in her ears. Kraarz and Freya waited patiently behind them.

Freya blushed as her stomach made an audible grumbling sound.

"Are you hungry?" the Shaman inquired.

Freya nodded.

"It feels like days since breakfast."

Kraarz smiled at her exaggeration and occupied himself with one of the many pouches hanging from his belt.

"I believe I have some honeybread here somewhere."

"That would be lovely."

There was a slight grating sound and Freya shrieked, but as Kraarz and Vox turned to find out why, she disappeared into a hole in the wall.

Vox bounded forward, its claws scrabbling as it slammed into the closed secret door, "Sweet Vaarzasia!"

Kraarz cursed in his own language.

Lin spun.

"Why didn't you two protect her?" she stood up, her hand dropping to the hilt of her sword.

"We did not have a chance, Lin. They took her before we knew they were there," Kraarz shrugged turning his hands palm up.

"Where would they take her?" Lin demanded.

Kraarz and Vox looked at each other and nodded simultaneously.

"The Prison."

"How in the name of Fiörna do we find that?" Lin demanded.

Vox grinned, his eyes narrowing and giving his fox-like face a definite wicked cast.

"I use my nose."

IN THE TOWER'S WINDOW, Freya was being strapped onto a massive cartwheel by two burly ogres.

"I must admit, I am surprised at her lack of struggle, Lord." Beside the red and black robed figure, a black stone jar with a single roiling, green eye, watched the scene, a lascivious smile on its lips.

The Aracan Katuvana shrugged.

"You do not seem happy that she has been captured so easily." The Jar's eye swivelled around the outside curve of its body as the Aracan Katuvana turned and stalked back to the throne.

He sat down with one gauntleted hand disappearing into the shadow of his hood and stared at the window.

Gmichi picked the Jar up and scurried across the room, depositing his burden on a pedestal beside the throne. The Jar alternated between watching the window and looking at the Aracan Katuvana.

In the window, the ogres had carried Freya and the wheel over to the wall and slid it onto a large axle poking out of the stones. Below the wheel sat a large trough. The wheel had been positioned with Freya lying horizontal above the glittering water and in which teamed a school of fish. They leapt and snapped at her left foot and hand, which were just inside the inner rim of the wheel.

"What are you planning, Lord? This introspection is most unlike you," the Jar murmured, frowning.

With a wave of his hand, the Aracan Katuvana increased the volume on the window...

"How in Tyr's name did I get myself into this?" the voluptuous girl groaned.

Securely lashed to the wheel on the wall of the Torture Chamber, Freya watched the approaching Dark Mistress with some trepidation.

"Forget how you got *yourself* into it; how did you get *me* into it!"

Across the chamber, the barred side of the holding cell allowed its occupants a ringside seat at the entertainments provided for the Dark Mistresses.

The current incumbent pressed himself up against the bars, an irritated expression on his handsome face.

The Dark Mistress paced ever closer, her silver plaits tipped with shining golden blades, that swayed with her sultry walk. She was clad in red leather, with a long skirt that had slits on both sides, showing legs with soft dark skin above thigh-high black leather boots.

Freya closed her eyes, hearing the tap, tap of the steel-heeled boots echo around the cavernous room.

"Now this is going to be good," the Jar said.

The Aracan Katuvana grunted and waved a hand at the Jar, who fell silent.

Chapter Nine

"If you hadn't run off ahead of us, you wouldn't have got captured," Freya retorted, watching the masked woman perusing a selection of instruments and whips hanging on a nearby rack.

"If you would just act the way a proper maiden should, I wouldn't have been in that position," Vrenstalliren hissed. "I was scouting ahead to make sure that there was nothing going to attack you."

"For the last time, Prince Vrenstalliren, I am not a maiden! How could I endure the life I have had to this point and still be a maiden?" Freya felt like strangling him with her bare hands. The amulet Kraarz had given her was in pieces on the floor, having fallen off while the wheel had been put in place and stood on by an ogre. *What was the point in guarding me against magic when I was abducted physically?*

The Dark Mistress turned and slapped Freya across the face, her sharpened nails leaving bloody furrows across Freya's cheek.

"You will not speak so to the next King of Alethdariel."

Vrenstalliren blinked and stared.

"My sister is next in line and my brother after her. I won't..." his voice trailed away, and he frowned.

The woman paced over to the bars, and slowly ran her fingers drown his bare chest.

"The Aracan Katuvana will not see such a fine specimen of Elven Royalty wasted." Blood from Freya's cheek inscribed lines over his skin.

"Do I know you?" He pulled away from her touch.

"You'll get to know me soon," she purred and reaching through the bars, grabbed the waistband of his leggings, pulling him towards her. "As soon as I have finished with my current task, you and I shall spend some quality time together."

Vrenstalliren threw himself backward, her nails ripping the material away from his body.

"No! I am a Paladin of Espilieth; your wiles cannot affect me."

She laughed and tossed the ruined leggings aside.

"I shall look forward to trying, though, your Grace." Her gaze lingered on his groin for a second before the Dark Mistress spun and stalked back to Freya.

"You have been such a very naughty girl," she said, her fingers delicately tracing the drying scratches on Freya's cheek. "You have upset some important people and now you will reap the reward of such disobedience."

Freya flinched.

"What do you mean? The only important people I know have all been happy with my efforts."

The Dark Mistress laughed.

"Those are in the past. The people you need to please now, are the ones watching every move you make." She stretched her arms and sighed. "But first we have to make you sorry for what you did."

Stepping to one side, the Dark Mistress pulled a lever, which started the wheel turning slowly.

Freya looked down and saw the water and the fish coming closer to her head. "I haven't done anything! I haven't hurt anyone or stolen anything. Why are you doing this?" Her hair started to dip into the water, the fish tugging on it eagerly.

"I do this because I am told to." She paused, and then giggled. "Of course, I enjoy it as well."

The ends of Freya's hair were almost touching the water. The fish jumped at it and Freya shrieked as several hairs were torn from her scalp by the eager piscines.

The Dark Mistress pressed a button and the wheel halted, squeaking.

"Are you sorry?"

"I haven't done anything!" Freya screamed as another fish leapt from the water and nipped the end of her nose.

"My babies are hungry today, it seems," the mistress smiled. "They only ate a Gremlin yesterday. I wonder what sort of mess they could make of that beautiful face of yours."

"No. Please, don't hurt me." Blood from her nose fell into the water, sending the fish into a feeding frenzy. "I don't understand why I'm here, or why you're doing this!"

The door to the Torture Chamber flew open.

"Halt!" A familiar voice bellowed, the Jinran accent rolling around the capacious room. "You shall not continue with this barbarity."

"Grald!" Freya squealed with delight.

The Mistress turned and hissed.

"You will not stop me, I am protected." She snapped her fingers; instantly they were surrounded by a group of Dragon Spawn.

They hissed and spat at Grald as he advanced, bared blade held high. One dragon spawn leapt at him and Grald knocked it away with his shield. The creature landed in the small pool and shrieked as the water bubbled around it.

"Hmm. Won't need to feed that shoal tonight," the Mistress laughed.

"Glad to be of service," Grald snarled, splitting a second Dragon Spawn in two with one blow.

"Watch out!" Vrenstalliren shouted as several dragon spawn appeared behind the knight.

Grald saluted the encaged Paladin and spun, slicing through three of the Spawn before they had moved.

Freya watched, entranced by her brother's skills with a sword. *How did he improve his sword work so much? It's hard to follow him while I hang upside down, but when he left Jira, he was only good in one on one, never melee. He always got knocked out in the arena battles.*

Another Dragon Spawn lunged at Grald and managed to grab his shield. He slammed it into a nearby column and dropped it down the opening of a pit. A roar echoed up from below and a shriek as whatever was in the pit devoured the dragon spawn.

"My, my. What a warrior we have here," the Dark Mistress purred to Freya. "He's too good for these idiots. I may have to take him on myself."

"He'll have you chopped into pieces before you can touch him," Vrenstalliren crowed from the holding cell. "You'll be gremlin fodder."

"Sadly, I think your companion may be right, my sweet prisoner," the Mistress said, running a nail along Freya's body. "But I have more than one trick up my tight leather sleeves."

"You won't get a..." Freya started. Her voice disappeared as the mistress held a black dagger to her throat, pressing hard enough for a dribble of blood to run from the blade and drip into the water, sending the fish into a second frenzy, jumping up, their fins splashing Freya's face with water, and tugging on her hair.

"...Chance?" the mistress finished her sentence, then whispered "Oh, my dear, I know more about your brother than you think I do. He'd never put you in danger."

How did she know Grald is my brother? Freya stared up at the woman.

Vrenstalliren threw his naked body at the bars.

"No! You will not harm my holy charge!"

Holy charge? Is that why he decided to accompany me... he'd been told to? Not because he'd fallen in love with me? Freya felt oddly annoyed. *I suppose I'm not that good at seduction after all.* Her heart constricted. *I was always told by customers that I was the best of Jetara's girls, that my massage skills and dancing were beyond compare, but maybe they were just being nice so that I'd be happy to sleep with them...* she felt a wave of sorrow at all the time she had spent in bed with otherwise ugly, elderly merchants and nobles.

"And what are you going to do about it?" the mistress sneered, her attention taken away from Freya for a moment.

The mistress' voice shocked Freya out of her self pity. *No! I am more than just "one of Jetara's girls" best of them or not! I will be more than that; I'm of the Bloodline of Elysian Empresses.*

She turned all the self pity into strength and bit into the arm that laid across her face, clenching her teeth as hard as she could and was rewarded with blood as she managed to penetrate the oddly thin leather.

The Mistress shrieked and snatched her arm away, dropping the dagger into the water below Freya.

Blood spurted out over Freya's face, and she spat her mouthful into the trough below. The fish swarmed on it gratefully.

"Bravo Freya!" Vrenstalliren cheered. "See that Grald? Your sister is..." his voice trailed away as the mistress laughed, even as she staunched the flow of blood from her arm with a spell.

Freya shook the woman's blood out of her eyes and looked up as she realised that the noise of the fight had stopped. The fish finished with the lump of flesh and resumed jumping and snapping at her face.

Grald sheathed his blade and strode across to the mistress, the dragon spawn making way for him.

"Are you okay?"

"Oh, Grald my Love. This is nothing," the mistress giggled. "You've given me worse wounds making love!"

Freya stared up at her brother, who had taken the mistress into his arms. *What's going on?*

"I know, but I don't like it when you get hurt in a battle. That was why you had the Dragon Spawn, remember?" Grald kissed the woman passionately.

"I'll be fine. Don't fuss," the dark mistress said breathlessly when he released her lips.

"What in Espilieth's name is going on, Grald?" Vrenstalliren shouted. "You were winning! You could have had us free in a few more moments."

Grald spun on the Paladin, a broad smile wreathing his face.

"Oh yes, I've defeated much harder enemies than this bunch." He gestured back at the remains of the Dragon Spawn squad who had gathered at the back of the torture chamber, cleaning their weapons on their tunics. "But free you? Now, that wasn't part of the plan."

Vrenstalliren's jaw dropped, and Freya gasped.

"What do you mean?"

Grald turned to her, his arm wrapped around the Dark Mistress's waist.

"This was supposed to be a surprise for you, Little Sister. How else was I going to introduce my wife to you?"

The Dark Mistress smiled and took off her mask.

"The idea was that I was to almost torture you and Grald would burst in, destroy the Dragon Spawn protecting me and rescue you. Then the three of us would have gone to Grald's quarters and celebrated." The face under the mask was of a stunning dark elf, her deep ebony skin making her pale gold eyes and silver hair stand out in the torchlight. She snapped her fingers and a gremlin appeared and turned the wheel, so Freya was upright. "I wouldn't have hurt my sister-in-law."

Freya looked at Grald who was beaming at his wife.

"Grald. Please, explain what's going on. Why are you married to a dark elf?"

"Haven't you figured it out yet? I thought you were at least capable of following an explanation," Vrenstalliren snorted. "He's one of them."

"Don't insult my sister, Elf," Grald snapped and flung one arm out. Blue lightning streaked across the room and slammed Vrenstalliren into the far wall of the holding cell. He screamed and smoke began to rise from his hair.

"Stop it Grald, you're hurting him!" Freya writhed against the grip of the straps on her limbs.

Grald stopped. "Yes, I was hurting him, wasn't I? But it's so much fun to have that much power, why shouldn't I use it?" he looked at his hand where lightning crackled across his knuckles and smiled.

When he looked up at her again, she saw a deep golden ring surrounding his pupil. *I'm sure that's never been there before...*

Freya stared at her older brother and wept helplessly.

"ARE WE THERE YET?" Lin asked.

"Would you stop asking that? I can't concentrate on what I am following if you keep talking," Vox snapped.

Lin looked at Kraarz and the blind Urakh grinned.

"Be at peace my friend. Vox is following a scent in the otherworld instead of following it directly..."

"This corridor leads all the way round the outside of the dungeon." Vox said absently.

"We're going the long way round?" Lin burst in. "Why? My Lady could be dead by the time we get there!"

Vox stopped and looked up at her.

"Lin, please be patient. The route I'm taking avoids the majority of the rooms in this dungeon and with a bit of luck, we'll reach the Prison without being detected."

Lin nodded and the Flixen started moving again, his black nose held to the floor.

"How much bigger is Vox going to get?" Lin asked Kraarz quietly. "He won't fit through the corridors if he gets much bigger, especially with that wingspan." She glanced up at the folded wings, the tips of the flight feathers brushing through cobwebs near the ceiling.

Kraarz held one hand out and Vox swished its tail, the black tip brushing across his palm. "Hmm. I'd say that he had another foot to full growth. But we'll be out of here before that happens."

At the next junction, Vox stopped.

"The prison is to the left." He sniffed the air and turned right.

"If the prison is to the left, why are we going right?" Lin halted and folded her arms. "I'm not moving any further unless you explain yourself."

Vox blew out an expressive breath and turned his head back over his shoulder to look at her. "She isn't there. Why would we go somewhere she isn't?"

"You said she was in the prison!"

"I was wrong." Vox shrugged. "It happens sometimes."

Lin sighed. "All right. Let's go." She slipped her sword out of its sheath.

"Good idea." Kraarz nodded approvingly and snapped his fingers. A ball of green fire appeared over the top of his staff.

The Flixen rolled his eyes. "There aren't any creatures around. I'd be able to feel them if there were."

"I thought you said that the Dark Gods shielded dungeons and their creatures from you?" Lin frowned. "Make your mind up."

"I don't have a mind, so how can I make it up?" Vox ignored her exasperated cry and moved forward again.

"Where do you think you two are going?" a voice asked from behind them.

"Two? Hello?" Vox blinked. "What about me?"

Lin spun round, the tip of her sword flying out to land in the throat of a large devil demon. A dribble of blue-black blood stained the steel and ran down the creature's upper body. She pulled back into a defensive stance.

He backed away.

"Steady on. I mean you no harm. I just wanted to know why one of our allies was in the company of an Outlander." The devil demon looked at Kraarz.

"My race turned from the Aracan Katuvana eons ago," the Shaman replied. "We found our freedom and a home without him."

The Devil Demon frowned; his golden cat slit eyes narrowed.

"Then you are an enemy; and the new Custodian was right."

"New Custodian, right? Right about what?" Vox asked.

The corpulent demon straightened his shoulders.

"Looks like I get to do a bit more training."

Kraarz and Lin had shifted positions gradually, Lin moving in front of Kraarz, but allowing him a clear view of the demon. She raised her sword and the demon grinned, flexing the long black claws on his hands.

"Come on then, Little Outlander. I'll snap you in half like a fresh femur."

"Oi!" Vox growled, pushed Lin aside and stalked right up to the demon, tail stiff. "Can you even see me, Blubber butt?" Vox tapped the demon with one huge paw, knocking him off balance and onto the floor.

"What the..." the demon looked around confused and Lin took her moment. Leaping over Vox, she landed, turned and sliced the demon's head off all in one smooth motion.

"Very well done, Lin," Kraarz applauded softly.

"I wouldn't have been able to do it without Vox pushing him over." Lin used the shaggy red fur on the demon's twitching legs to clean her sword.

"The demon couldn't see me," Vox tilted his head to one side. "Vaarzasia, Hel and Fiör created this body for me. Maybe they have made me invisible to the creatures of the Dark Gods?"

Lin hid a smile at Vox's confusion.

"Maybe they wanted you to realise that you aren't the centre of everyone's attention all the time."

Vox growled at her and stalked away down the corridor.

Kraarz and Lin followed, laughing.

Chapter Ten

"So, Lord. What do you wish to do now?" the Jar asked as the window faded to black. "All the pieces are in place, and we are already minus a Devil Demon, thanks to Goraln's slothfulness."

The Aracan Katuvana appeared to ponder the question for some time, then he shrugged and gestured.

The Lych Mistress appeared on the Window.

"I am almost ready, my most wonderful Lord." The Mistress curtseyed, her cleavage almost falling out of the low-necked purple gown she wore.

"Excellent," the Jar said. "However, the Lord needs you to do one more thing for him."

"Anything for my Betrothed."

"Send your Devil Demon to Jinra Dungeon. That fool Theraldin was too soft and let Goraln get out of shape." The Jar spat green goo at the floor. "It's just as well he's dead." A Gremlin appeared beside the pedestal and cleared up the goo.

The Lych Mistress made a note on a piece of parchment and passed it to a Gremlin who spun on the spot and disappeared.

"Lord Iniran will be there shortly, my Lord."

"Thank you. Our Lord looks forward to greeting you in the flesh," the Jar said.

The Lych Mistress curtseyed again and the Aracan Katuvana cleared the window. Then he stared at the Jar.

"What?" the Jar looked at the hooded figure. "I merely invited her over for a...getting-to-know-you-again meal." The Jar looked back at the window and with a whisper of power activated it. "Shall we see how our young empress is getting on?"

The Aracan Katuvana nodded and turned to the window.

AT LEAST I'M A BIT more comfortable now, Freya thought as she stared across the table at her brother. *The ball and chain are preferable to having my head dunked in flesh eating fish.*

"And that is how Erendell and I met and fell in love." Grald smiled at his wife, who was busy slicing up meat and bread.

"Very sweet." Freya didn't even try to keep the sarcasm out of her voice. "Why did you have to become a Dark Paladin though? Surely, she would have fallen for you as a good knight."

Erendell turned to look at her, her golden eyes gleaming molten in the lamplight.

"Never. I have been a follower of the Aracan Katuvana for many hundreds of years. Your brother would never have had a chance with me," she laughed.

"Besides which, I enjoy it." Grald looked at his hand, which sparkled with red flame. "I always did struggle with the honour required of a Gladiator Slave, not to mention having to lead raids for Lord Southnra. Only the thought of your fate should I break the rules, kept me from enjoying my kills."

Erendell put the food on the table between them and massaged Grald's shoulders.

"Now you can enjoy it as much as you want. The Aracan Katuvana only wishes results; he doesn't care how he gets them."

Freya dropped her eyes as they kissed passionately. *I have to get out of here. Where are the others?*

"Eat up, Little Sister. You and Erendell are going to get to know each other, and you'll need all your strength for that." Grald poured her a goblet of deep red wine.

"What are you going to do?" Freya ignored the wine.

"Sadly, my resident Devil demon was decapitated by your friends. I've been sent a temporary replacement, so he and I are going to deal with the problem." He swallowed deeply from his own goblet.

Freya's heart leapt. *They're alive!*

"Then I have to deal with your 'champion' in the holding cell," Grald finished.

"Please, allow us to deal with him." Erendell said. "Your sister will need someone to take out her *frustration* on and we do have orders to take him alive."

Grald nodded.

"Excellent notion, My Love. I'll leave it to you then." He smiled and looked at the laden table in front of them. "Shall we eat now? It'll be the first family dinner we've had together for ages."

Freya forced a smile onto her face.

"Of course, big brother." She picked up her goblet. "To my big brother, the one who always rescues me."

Grald's smile broadened.

"Thank you, I'm glad you noticed."

Erendell laughed and the two of them drank together.

Freya sipped from her goblet, recognised the tingle of a familiar drug and put it down to eat. *That's the compliance cocktail Jetara used to use. I need to eat to mitigate the effects. I just hope that Lin and the others get me out of here before it takes full hold.*

"THE HOLDING CELL IS just up here," Vox said when they caught up with it at a heavily barred oak door.

Lin rolled her head on her neck, easing the strain from the fight they'd just had.

"How did you get through the guard post without fighting?"

"I just walked through," Vox shrugged.

"You could have helped us." She frowned at him.

"But you and Kraarz seemed to be having so much fun with the skeletons that I didn't want to interfere."

Lin's face flushed.

"Peace, Lin." Kraarz patted Lin on the arm. "That was a difficult fight, Vox. We needed your help."

"Just because I help you sometimes, doesn't mean I should fight your battles for you."

Lin contented herself with scowling at the nonchalant Flixen and pushed the door open. She recoiled at the scent of decomposing flesh and sour blood that rolled out on the steam.

"What in Calliale's name?"

There was a flash of bright blue light and a tiny transparent hummingbird appeared in front of her.

"It's about time," the bird said, its wings a blur. *"Don't you know we deities have to be called upon to help humans?"*

Lin bowed her head.

"I apologise, Lady Calliale. I did not know you were intending to help us."

"So, my show with the hawk fell on deaf ears, huh." The hummingbird charged at Lin's face, stopping just in front of her nose. *"Typical. The Empress is in danger, and you are going the wrong way. If you don't get her out of here by sundown, our Nemesis shall have gained another willing servant and a foothold in Elysia."*

Kraarz raised white eyes to the bird. "Lady Goddess, we thank you for this instruction, but how are we to get her out of here unscathed? I suspect that the Custodian of this Dungeon will be here to deal with us in force shortly."

"It seems that Urakhs are becoming as dense as humans. Vox, you were given that body for a reason. Use it." The hummingbird circled Vox's head. *"I cannot stay much longer, or I shall bring too much danger upon*

your heads. Rescue the Empress and get her out of here by sundown." The bird disappeared.

Lin looked at Vox. "What did that mean?"

"I don't know." The Flixen looked puzzled. "Look, let's go look in here and I'll see if I can figure out what I've been given." He padded in through the door, steam billowing out around him. "It's all clear!" he called back.

Lin and Kraarz followed.

"My goddess!" Lin coughed as a wave of foul-tasting smoke blew over her. "Have we stepped into the punishment circles of the Netherworld?"

"I believe I would have felt it if we had," Kraarz snorted. He sniffed the thick smoke and steam clogged air. "No. This is one of the Aracan Katuvana's Torture Chambers." He drew a deep breath, catching a hint of familiar perfume and smiled. "Our Lady has been here and left, but we have the chance to rescue another companion."

"I know. I can see him," Vox snapped and bounded across the cavernous room.

"He always has to throw that into my face," Kraarz said sadly. "However, as I can see in other ways, the situation is not a difficulty."

There was a crash as Vox cut the holding cell bars in four with two quick swipes of its front paws.

Lin and Kraarz hurried over.

"A little bit noisy, but effective," Vox said, examining his claws. "No damage to my claws at all and the bars are solid steel."

"Are you trying to get us killed?" Vrenstalliren snapped from the back of the cell.

Kraarz rummaged around in one of his many pouches and produced a suit of leather hunting gear. "Here, I took your spare set from Ohtár's saddlebags. Something told me you might need them."

Vrenstalliren dressed hurriedly.

"No chance of you having a sword in there is there?"

"Sadly, no," the Urakh shrugged.

"I saw your weaponry in the Guard room," Lin said. "I just didn't realise it was yours."

"Thank Espilieth for that." The Paladin started to push past Vox, but the massive Flixen growled at him.

"Don't move," Vox sniffed the air. "We're about to have company."

"Control your creature, Urakh. Let's go get Freya." Vrenstalliren tried to push past again.

"There's someone coming, Sir Vrenstalliren," Kraarz told him. "Vox told you not to move."

"Wonderful." Vrenstalliren flexed his hands. "I have some revenge to exact."

"Don't be stupid, elf!" Vox snapped. "If I'm right about the abilities this body has been given, we should be able to get out of here without fighting." He turned towards the cell. "Lin, Kraarz, get in the corner with the elf prince and sit still."

Kraarz and Lin started to move, but Vrenstalliren stood his ground.

"We have to get me a weapon, I can't fight with my bare hands like a commoner," the elf prince objected, but Vox pushed him into a corner of the holding cell with one wing tip. "I told you to control your pet, Urakh."

Lin sighed. "Vox doesn't make it easy."

Kraarz laughed. "He never did. You just never had to work with him in physical form before. We'd best do as he says." He moved over beside Vrenstalliren and sat on the floor, pulling the elf down beside him.

Lin sat the other side of Vrenstalliren and Vox sat in front of them.

"I'm going to enclose you in my wings. I don't have a huge wingspan just yet, so you can't move."

"What is the creature doing?" Vrenstalliren started, trying to stand up. "If there are creatures of evil coming, then I should fight them in Espilieth's name. Give me your sword, woman."

"No one uses my blade, but me." Lin held back a laugh at the look on his face. "You chose the wrong goddess to become a Paladin of. Espilieth only helps with healing and magic. If you wanted aid in fighting, then you should have chosen Tyr or Fiörna."

The elven prince spluttered. "What are you trying to say?"

"Shush! They're here," Vox hissed at them.

Through the steam and smoke, Lin saw Grald stride in. He wore black burnished armour, and carried a massive bastard sword, blade bared, against his shoulder.

Lin blinked. "Looks like Vox is right about him then," she whispered to Kraarz, touching his hand.

"I'm always right about people's souls. I can see the state of them, remember?" Vox said in her mind. *"Quiet."*

Around Grald swarmed a hundred or so dragon spawn and behind him rose the tall black horns of a Devil Demon.

"Another one. Damn," Vox growled in their minds.

"Fan out, search everywhere. My senses say they haven't left the dungeon, so find them," Grald commanded, using the tip of his sword as a pointer.

The Devil Demon moved up beside Grald. His golden eyes gleamed with intelligence and his body looked as hard as polished Redstone.

"No chance of tricking this one," Lin said. *"He's obviously one of their better devil demons."*

"He has not succumbed to the greed of the demon half either," Kraarz added.

Vrenstalliren saw the demon and his eyes went flat, "I will not allow filth like that to bestride the world."

"Shhh," Lin whispered. "I don't know how far Vox's invisibility will shield us."

"You figured it out then, Lin," Vox said, sending an image of a smile to her.

Lin rolled her eyes and held onto Vrenstalliren's arm stopping him from moving.

The three companions held their breath as four Dragon Spawn examined the cut holding cell bars. One took a sample back to Grald who looked at it and passed it to the devil demon.

"Interesting. Clearly cut by an animal's claws and yet, I know of no animal living that could do such a thing." The devil demon's voice carried clearly across to them.

"If you could name any animal that could do it?" Grald asked, impatience colouring his voice.

"Any? Well, it would have to be the Sabre Toothed Flixaren. Our Forest Flixen and the Alethdanian Plains Flixen are related to them," the demon smiled, and Lin shuddered at the shreds of flesh between his teeth. "Sadly, the Sabre Toothed Flixaren died out many thousands of years ago, during the War of The Gods."

"I don't need a history lesson, Iniran. What does it look like?" Grald barked, swinging his blade round to the demon's chest.

"I was getting to that." Iniran sounded hurt. "It's six foot long with white fur, black stripes and wings. It has claws stronger than steel and if there is one in here, then we wouldn't see it."

"Why?" Grald ground the word out from beneath his teeth.

"The Gods of Light created it as a stealth assassin. It is invisible to Dark Creatures," the demon told him.

"And how do you know what it looks like if it's invisible to us?" the Dark Paladin appeared to be getting annoyed.

"You humans have a wonderful curiosity, and you write your findings down. I read the description in a book." Iniran smiled. "Wonderful things books."

"A reading Devil Demon? That's a first." Grald turned his back on him to watch the dragon spawn's efforts.

Iniran rolled his eyes and stopped talking.

The Dragon Spawn finished their search and reported back to Grald. He slapped several around the head and sent them back to their lair.

"Nothing. Whatever it was that cut the bars must have eaten Vrenstalliren and scarpered. There's no sign of Lin or her Urakh friend either."

"What now?" Iniran looked relived as Grald sheathed his sword.

"Back to the Dais Room." Grald rolled his shoulders. "If they are going to appear anywhere, it will be there. Take out the crystal and the dungeon collapses remember?"

Lin and Vrenstalliren exchanged an excited look. They waited until the room was clear, then Vox stood up and folded his wings back.

"You're up to full growth now, Vox," Kraarz commented, struggling to rise. Vrenstalliren helped the Shaman to his feet. "Thank you, your Highness."

"Now I know what I am." Vox grinned showing long curving canines the size of short swords. "I know what I can do."

"Nice body, Vox," Lin said, stroking the back of the Flixaren's head. He purred and almost knocked her off her feet, rubbing his head against her.

"I don't know where you picked your pet up, Lin, but he's very useful," Vrenstalliren said. "But, why do you keep talking to him as if he's more than just an animal?"

Vox growled at the elf and Vrenstalliren stepped away from him.

"Vrenstalliren, Kraarz and I can understand Vox's language and if you want to stay on his good side, I suggest you keep your mouth shut." Lin folded her arms and glared at him.

"All right," Vrenstalliren grumbled.

They moved out of the torture chamber and into the guardroom. The skeletons hadn't been replaced yet, so Vrenstalliren retrieved his weapons and shield.

"Right then," he said. "Let's go get that crystal and take this accursed place down."

"Not until we have rescued Lady Freya," Lin said firmly.

The elven prince rolled his eyes.

"I can feel the crystal they spoke of," Vox said. "And I can sense Freya; she's near there too."

"Then we get to kill two birds with one stone," Kraarz smiled.

Chapter Eleven

Freya stared up into the pulsing red heart shaped crystal hanging between the four gilded pillars on the dais. It spun and sparkled, the throbbing almost mimicking her heartbeat. *It's so gorgeous. How can someone evil create something so wonderful?*

"Beautiful, isn't it?" Erendell said. "This is just part of the power of the Aracan Katuvana, the heart of his dungeons and the life within his veins. It rewards those of us who follow him with eternal life."

Freya said nothing, content to watch the hypnotic pulse.

"Soon, you will be with us in heart and mind, one with your brother and I. Then I will truly be able to embrace you and call you sister." The dark elf took Freya's hand and drew her up the dais steps to stand in front of the crystal.

From that close, Freya could feel the warmth radiating out of the crystal. It sent a mild shiver of bliss through her body, and she gasped.

"Touch it," Erendell urged. "The effect is so much more pleasurable when you touch it."

Freya raised her left hand. Red energy jumped from the crystal to her hand, making her shiver with delight. *It couldn't hurt to touch it just once, could it?*

Erendell watched with an intense gleam in her golden eyes, and then she shuddered and felt herself shunted aside as the Aracan Katuvana took control of her body.

"Touch it, Freya. Touch it and know my love," the Aracan Katuvana said through Erendell.

Freya blinked and half turned to see that Erendell's pale gold eyes were now completely gold, a deep burnished red gold colour from lid to lid. She frowned.

"You're my brother's wife."

"Does that mean that I can't love you too?" Erendell/the Aracan Katuvana raised one hand and stroked Freya's cheek softly. "Why shouldn't I love both sister and brother? Our Lord doesn't mind." She ran her hand down her shoulder, over Freya's breast and along her right arm, gently taking her hand and holding the palm out toward the crystal. "Touch my Crystal, Freya and become one with me."

Freya pulled away.

"You aren't Erendell. She doesn't like me. I'm competition for Grald's love."

"You are correct. I'm not Erendell, but all of my servants are well rewarded for serving me thus." The Aracan Katuvana laughed and Erendell's body shook in the throes of an orgasm. "See? I am not uncaring to my people."

Freya placed her hands on her hips, feeling along the leather belt she wore around her waist.

"I will never serve you. I won't place the fate of my people in your hands." She backed away, only to come up short against a pillar. As she moved, she slipped her fingers through the hilt loops of the tiny dagger secreted in her belt buckle.

"I see you have accepted what your companions have told you." The Aracan Katuvana laughed again. "But you will serve me, Freya. One way or another you will serve me."

"I can't serve you dead." Freya slipped the dagger free and held it to her heart. "This might not be long, but it is sharp, and you don't need much more than an inch of blade to penetrate the heart"

The Aracan Katuvana laughed, bending Erendell double with mirth.

"You dying will not stop me. I can return those I wish from the Otherworld. As I did with Princess Loriel, I can bring you back to life and make you mine. Or I can just install Grald onto the Empire's throne. Either way, I win."

"You shall never win!" Vrenstalliren shouted from the door. "Get away from my Lady! In Espilieth's name I challenge you!"

The Aracan Katuvana turned Erendell to look at the elven prince.

"Fool. As if I would waste a valuable resource to bring you to your knees." Erendell snapped her fingers and Iniran appeared beside the dais. "Get him," the Aracan Katuvana commanded. "But do not kill him. I have plans for him as well."

Freya sighed with relief as Vrenstalliren stepped into the room to engage the Devil Demon. She saw Vox creep in and circle around behind the fight. *"You came for me at last!"*

"I couldn't leave you here. You're important to Lin and Kraarz." The massive creature paused for a moment. *"And anyway, I like you. You smell good and your skin is soft."*

Freya giggled.

Lin followed Vox into the room and Kraarz stopped in the doorway, obviously guarding from intrusion. Lin tried to slip around the perimeter of the room, but Erendell turned toward her.

"Oh no you don't, Elysian. This pretty one will be mine," the Aracan Katuvana snarled and Erendell snapped her fingers again, summoning a handful of assorted creatures from the Lair just beyond the Dais Room.

Grald followed the creatures in and lounged in the doorway, smiling at Freya as if they were alone.

"So, how do you like the place, Little Sister? Fancy becoming a member of the Aracan Katuvana's family?"

"No. I would never join with such evil. I'm still surprised that you did." She blinked back tears. "Mama always thought you were a good boy."

"Our parents were outlawed by our grandmother, Freya. We were ejected from our own country before *you* were born. Besides, if Papa had not been away when the Slavers attacked, we might still have had a family."

Freya looked at him.

"What do you mean? I thought Papa was dead?"

He shrugged.

"You were but a babe in arms, what else should I tell you? He left Mama to go to Jira and find work. The slavers attacked that evening."

Freya felt hope leap in her heart.

"Is he still alive?"

"I don't know, and I don't care. I have my own family now." Grald stood up and approached the dais, dodging the gremlin that was flung past him by Lin. "Papa never tried to find us. Join my family; let us be happy together again. Just touch the crystal with both hands."

Lin beheaded a Demon Spawn, shouting, "My Lady! Don't do it."

Vox leapt and knocked Grald to the floor, sending him flying into Iniran's legs and making the devil demon stagger.

"Your father is alive. He lives in Elyandor! Help us get to that crystal and destroy this dungeon."

Vrenstalliren took advantage of the pause in his fight to incant.

"Espilieth, shirrailer ennis!"

A bright white bubble of light enclosed Freya, Lin and himself.

The Devil demon laughed and flung himself forward to grapple with the knight.

"Your pretty little goddess' shield cannot hurt a follower of Tzeentch!" Smoke began to curl up from the demon's skin as the holy shield scorched him.

"Maybe his goddess can't, but I can," Vox roared, and he jumped and planted his forepaws onto the devil demon's back. Then he let his claws out and ripped his paws down, sending blue-black blood spurting through the air.

Iniran screamed and spun, trying to see where his attacker was. Vrenstalliren recovered quickly enough to swing his sword and relieve the devil demon of his head. The creature's blood fountained up, splashing over everyone in the vicinity. The body toppled and fell knocking Grald over again.

The barbarian knight pushed himself up, wiping demon blood from his face.

"Wasn't my devil demon," he muttered as he regained his feet. Then he smiled. "However, he was the Aide of my Mistress, Lady Lych herself and my Lord has never liked losing his followers, so it lies upon me to revenge his death upon you."

"Gladly do I accept such a challenge, false knight." Vrenstalliren brought his sword up.

The two men began to duel.

Erendell spun and grabbed Freya, her sharpened nails clutching her throat.

"Stop fighting and she lives," the Aracan Katuvana said calmly, his voice penetrating the noise of battle around them. "I need the elf prince alive, Grald. I would rather not kill your sister, either."

Smoke began to rise from Erendell's skin as the Aracan Katuvana pushed against the holy shield.

Grald's eyes widened.

"My Lord! No, please..." He stopped fighting and moved toward the dais, one hand extended toward Erendell, the other sheathing his sword.

Vrenstalliren followed Grald, his sword still bare, but before he could do anything else, a patrol of skeletons surrounded him, forcing him to mind his own defences.

Freya brought her dagger up and pushed its tip sharply into Erendell's hip.

The pain shocked Erendell and she screamed, pulling away. The Aracan Katuvana's possession released her, she staggered backward down the dais stairs and dropped to the floor, one hand clutching her hip.

Grald rushed forward and caught her, laying her gently down on the floor. He checked the wound and sighed.

"It's not serious. Good."

Vrenstalliren finished off his attackers, before he moved between Grald and Freya. Vox padded to Freya's side standing between her and the crystal.

"Looks like your sister saved your wife's life," Kraarz said, picking his way across the floor with his staff.

Lin killed the last of the creatures assailing her and joined Freya on the dais, holding her blade dripping with ichor in front of the girl, its point toward Grald.

"Please, Freya. Come and be my sister again." Grald looked at her. "Join us."

"Tell me one thing," Freya said. "Why did you become one of the Aracan Katuvana's creatures?"

He looked at Erendell who lay on the floor. Then he looked at Freya again.

"It was the only way I could free you from slavery. I wouldn't have left the Castle Grof dungeon alive, so I bargained with the only thing I had left."

Tears ran down Freya's cheeks.

"Graldai..." she stepped toward him.

"Well, this is all very nice, but we have a job to do," Vox snapped.

The Flixaren whirled and sliced one of the pillars in half with his massive claws. The top half crashed down and rolled over Erendell who screamed.

"No! How did you do that?" Grald glared at Kraarz who shrugged.

"I didn't. Vox did," the Urakh said matter-of-factly as the distraught dark Paladin struggled to remove the gilded column from his wife's legs.

Vox moved to the next pillar.

"Kraarz, come here. You'll need an empty bag. Don't let the crystal touch your skin."

Kraarz moved over, pulling a sack out from one of his pouches. Vrenstalliren and Lin stayed between Grald and Freya as she moved away from the crystal.

Unable to move the column, Grald held his wife's head as she died, murmuring softly into her ears and stroking her face. As Erendell sighed her last and closed her eyes, Grald kissed her and laid her head down.

Then he stood up and pulled his sword from its sheathe with a steely hiss.

"You have taken away my only love. I will never forgive you this, Freya."

"I didn't do anything!" she said.

Vrenstalliren moved forward.

"Advance no further. You might be my Lady's brother, but that shall not stay my blade a second time."

"Foolish elf," his opponent growled. "You are no match for me, and I swear now in the name of Kaela Mensha, despite my orders, if you dare cross blades with me again, you will die."

"I fight in Espilieth's name, and she shall guide my blade." At his words, a white flame surrounded his blade, burning away the blue-black blood of the devil demon staining the steel.

"So be it." Grald swung his massive blade in a circle, aiming for Vrenstalliren's knee. "As my Lord is watching, I shall attempt to keep the damage of your flesh to a minimum, so that you may be reanimated the way Princess Loriel was."

Vrenstalliren blocked the blow. "My sister is dead, fiend. She has been dead for over a hundred years."

"She was reanimated and has become the Aracan Katuvana's most trusted servant," Grald sneered, aiming for the elven prince's shield arm. Vrenstalliren raised his shield to block the blow. "She was the one who persuaded me that this way was better." His sword ripped through the plated steel shield like it was cloth and cleaved Vrenstalliren's arm in two.

Freya gasped.

Lin watched the fight clinically. "He's not going to survive this."

"Vox, get the bedamned crystal free quickly!" Kraarz said.

The Flixaren cut a second pillar in half, jumping over the stump.

"Why won't it fall?"

"You probably need to do a third one." Kraarz pointed at the one beside him.

"Get out of the way then."

Kraarz moved so that he was under the crystal, his sack held open wide.

Vox swiped at the post, its claws passing through the stone and gilding like a diver into a lake. The fourth column quivered and crumbled into dust, as the crystal stopped pulsing and dropped.

Kraarz caught it neatly in the sack.

"Let us remove the Empress from this sordid place."

Lin glanced back at them.

"We have to wait." She waved one hand at the battle between the knights.

"It's nearly sundown, Lin," Vox said. "Let me take Freya and Kraarz out and I'll come back for you."

Lin nodded.

"A good idea."

"No! I have to wait for Vrenstalliren." Freya struggled as Lin pulled her back towards Vox. Kraarz had already mounted the Flixaren's back, holding the sack with the crystal in front of him.

"I'll wait for him, I promise. Just get Kraarz out of here," Lin lowered her voice. "He's getting old and needs more help than he admits."

Freya nodded and reluctantly climbed up behind the Urakh.

"Make sure you and Vrenstalliren survive, Lin."

"I'll try," Lin said, backing away as Vox beat his wings and took off. Lin looked up at the high ceiling, following the travellers.

Vox waved a paw, and then winked out in a flash of light. Lin smiled and turned back to the fight.

Grald howled in anger as he saw Freya and Kraarz disappear in mid air.

"You are not getting away from me that easily, Little Sister." He swung his sword with both hands.

Vrenstalliren parried as quickly as he could, but the force of the blow, combined with his weakening grip made his sword fly out of his hand. The blow continued through and sliced into the elven prince, but the blade stuck in his armour and Grald had to rip it from the elf's body without killing him.

The elf prince collapsed on the stairs, not far from Frendell, gasping for breath.

"You still live and thus I have followed my orders," Grald smiled. "Now I can find my sister again." He looked around the room, thinking.

Vrenstalliren's sword had landed near Lin's feet. She stooped quickly and snatched it up.

"Now that she is away and safe, I can deal with you," she said as he turned toward her.

"And what can you do, Elysian. I am the emperor. You will bow to me," Grald said.

"The throne passes only to the male line when there is no female line. Your sister always has been the Heir Presumptive." Lin spun Vrenstalliren's sword in a figure eight to test the weight, then drew her own sword again, holding it in her other hand.

"Then I shall have to make sure there is no female line!" Grald surged forward and Lin danced out of the way.

"You will have to kill all your cousins then. I had to make sure that your mother or sister wasn't alive before I could pass it to your aunt's daughters." She laughed and dodged another blow. "They will be disappointed that they don't get to fight over who inherits."

"The Aracan Katuvana will aid me." Grald spun, letting the weight of his sword do most of the work. "But first I have to get rid of you and then my sister."

Lin leaned back to let the blade fly past her waist and then slid in behind him. Dropping her sword, she plunged Vrenstalliren's into Grald's side, angling it upward to hit his heart.

"You are a worthy opponent, but Vrenstalliren's injuries require recompense that will only be paid for by your death. So, to lessen my Lady's suffering, I give you a fast death." She felt his heart throbbing on the tip of the sword.

Grald gasped and staggered back against her, dropping his bastard sword uselessly to the floor. Lin finally got a close look at his face and was surprised to see a thin golden ring around his pupils, the rest of his eyes were brown. As she twisted the sword and his heart burst, the golden ring disappeared.

Letting him fall to the floor, she left the sword in him and returned to Vrenstalliren.

"I killed him for you."

"Thank you," the knight said.

Looking at his ruined body, she wondered how he had managed to stay alive after that blow. "Will your goddess aid you?"

"No. She will ease my end though." He sighed and closed his eyes.

Lin felt tears rolling down her cheeks as the dungeon began to rumble.

VOX REAPPEARED IN THE clearing where the horses were. Kore galloped over to Freya as she fell off Vox's back. *"You are back safely!"*

"Yes," she told him sadly. "I'm safe."

Kraarz slid off Vox's back.

"Where is there a patch of sunlight?"

Freya looked around, then grabbed Kraarz and dragged him over beside the pool.

"This is the only patch left. The sun will be out of view in moments."

"I had best work quickly."

"This is why we had to get out of there by sundown," Vox told them. "Hurry up and expose the crystal to the sunlight."

Kraarz opened the bag and let the sun fall onto the quiescent red crystal. Almost immediately, the ground began to shake. Rocks tumbled from the top of the waterfall and the horses reared in fear.

"I'll calm them down," Kore said and galloped back.

There was a screech from the cave as more rocks rolled down to block the entrance.

"Vox, go get Lin and Vrenstalliren!" Freya yelled.

Vox leapt into the air, but as he began to beat his wings, a massive boulder tumbled over the cliff edge above and landed on his back. Vox slammed into the water, showering Kraarz and Freya.

"Vox!" Freya screamed.

The red crystal faded slowly to clear. The rumbling stopped and Kraarz held a hand over the remaining clear crystal.

"I can sense power, but not evil."

"That's because it is the Aracan Katuvana's blood that taints the crystals and bind their power to him." A familiar voice said in their minds. *"Put it away."*

Freya turned to look at Kraarz. Floating above his shoulder was Vox in its normal spirit ball form. "So, you didn't get Lin out then."

Kraarz smiled and retied the neck of the sack.

"Did it look like I had a chance to? My mortal body was crushed and drowned. It's lucky that we spirits are immortal." Vox flew over to her and hovered in front of her. *"Let's go back to the Cuddly Cub. I think you and Kraarz need some rest."*

"But Lin?" Freya protested. "And Vrenstalliren?"

Kraarz took Ohtár's reins and pulled himself up onto the white mare's saddle.

"That sounds like a good idea. Lady Lin has removed herself from many tight spots. I have confidence that she will find us."

Chapter Twelve

Freya stroked Kore's nose, *"I can't believe that my brother became so evil."*

"From the story you told me, he did it to free you and then couldn't free himself." The stallion tossed his head.

"Are you all right, my Lady?" Kraarz asked as he entered the stable yard.

She turned, "Has Vox come back yet?"

"No, but he often disappears for days." Kraarz sat down on a bale of straw.

"I suppose there is no hope now," Freya sniffed, and Kore nuzzled her cheek.

"There is always hope," the big stallion said. *"Do you want to go for a ride?"*

"No thank you, Kore," she sighed.

"Why is your aura so sad?" Vox said, appearing over Kore's head.

"Because Lin didn't survive the collapse of the Dungeon," Freya replied, then did a double take, "Vox!"

"Are you sure?" The ball of light bounced around Freya.

"I don't know anyone who could have survived that kind of underground collapse." She replied, sadly.

"Well, you do now," a tired voice said. Lin limped into the stable yard, covered in dirt.

"How?" Freya rushed up to her and hugged her.

Lin winced. "I dug my way out."

"But..."

"Give me a chance to have a bath and get some healing and I'll tell you," she said, looking at the dirt caking her hands.

"Oh, of course. I'll meet you in the common room then."

"Get a private dining room. I'm rather hungry." Lin squeezed Freya in a one armed hug and limped into the tavern. Vox flew after her.

"Vox will heal her," Kraarz said, coming up beside Freya.

"Then we'd better get her something to eat." Freya grinned at the Urakh Shaman. "Got any more of those cartwheel sized gold coins?"

One of the Elysian coins gave them a veritable feast as well as the use of the only private dining room. Freya and Kraarz sipped warmed spiced wine, while Lin drank only water during her recitation of the events after they had left the dungeon. Vox floated above an unlit candle just in case someone walked in.

"So, you released my brother from his soul contract to the Aracan Katuvana?" Freya frowned. "How?"

"How do you think?" Vox said, its light flashing red for a moment.

Freya blinked and looked from Vox to Lin who sighed and nodded.

Tears began to run down Freya's cheeks, and she bit her lip, "There was no other way?"

"Part of the spell on the crystal binds the Custodian to the dungeon. He would have died when the crystal was cleansed anyway." Vox paused. *"And believe me; death by sword is quicker and gentler than the spell withdrawal would have been."*

Freya shrugged, "I'll take your word for it," she sniffed and wiped her nose on the back of her hand. "So, what happened to Vrenstalliren?"

"Espilieth took his soul with her. She told me to give his sword to Kraarz, because Kraarz has another task to do and needs to get to Alethdariel by midwinter." She passed the clean and sheathed sword across to Kraarz. "Vox is going with you."

"I welcome the opportunity to see more of this wonderful land, but how am I to cover such a distance in such a short time?" Kraarz shook his head. "It would take me half a year to walk that far south."

"Vrenstalliren gave me Ohtár. He said you could have his mare, her name is Swiftwind." Lin smiled, "She knows the way home. There is one condition though."

"And that is?" Kraarz shrugged. "I will do whatever it is, for it is a dying man's last wish."

"Vrenstalliren is... was betrothed to Lady Julissa Alethdan. He asked that you give her this gift, from him." Lin passed over a soft leather wrapped bundle. Kraarz put it into one of his many pouches.

They ate in silence for a while, each wrapped in their own thoughts.

"So, what do we do now?" Freya asked, sipping her wine.

"I am going south to Alethdariel." Kraarz said.

"I know that; I meant for me." Freya sighed and put her cup down on the table.

"You and I will ride to Elyandor and see if we can find your father. While we are there, we shall raise an army to help the heart kingdoms in their fight." Lin finished her water.

"How do I do that? If what you have told me is right, my aunt and cousins will be sceptical that I am the heir," Freya said.

"You have a point," Lin mused. "When your family left, your mother took the jewels your grandfather gave her. The Elysian Seal Ring was amongst them, much to your grandmother's displeasure." Lin looked at Freya. "Do you have any of your mother's jewels?"

"Grald took most of them with him when he was freed." She frowned. "However, I found something on the way to meet him."

"What?" Lin looked hopeful.

"One of grandfather's treasure boxes. It had a ring box that my mother showed me once. I'll go get it." Freya stood and disappeared up the stairs to the rooms. She returned quickly with the red Graistun box and opened it to reveal the gold ring box.

"That looks familiar," Lin said.

"I thought it might have been mother's engagement ring. I haven't had any time to look at it." Freya took a deep breath and touched the button to open the ring box.

The smaller box popped open easily to reveal three rings.

"This was mother's engagement ring," Freya said, picking up a small gold ring bearing an emerald surrounded by diamonds. She sniffed and blinked away tears. "The last time I saw it I was a toddler." She slipped it onto her right hand and picked up a smooth silver coloured ring. It had gems set into the top of the band and would only fit on Freya's thumb. "I think this was Grandfather's." She took it off again and put it back into the box.

The third ring had a huge ruby cabochon set into it. The face of the cabochon was carved with a wingless dragon.

"I've never seen this before."

"I have," Lin gasped. "That's the Seal Ring. Only the true heir to the throne can wear it." She looked intently into Freya's face. "Put it on your left index finger."

Freya looked at it, doubt colouring her tone, "The band is too small."

"It has a spell on it; it will resize itself," Lin said. "Put it on."

The girl shrugged and picked it up, sliding it onto her finger. There was a flash of light from within the stone that blinded Freya and Lin momentarily.

Freya blinked until she could see again and looked down at the ring.

"You were right, it fits perfectly." Then she looked down at the stone again. "It's flashing."

"Pulsing," Lin corrected her. "Only those with the full blood royal can wear it; for anyone else it is too small and stays a plain ruby. Take it off for the moment; we'll use it to make your case when we reach Elyandor and your father."

"What about my cousins?" Freya said, putting the seal back into the ring box, closing it and placing the ring box into the Graistun one. "Won't they be able to wear it as well?"

"It depends on the strength of the blood royal in their veins." Lin replied smiling. She poured herself some wine, topping up Kraarz and Freya's cups, "And there are rumours that it isn't as strong as their mother asserts."

She sipped from her cup then raised it, "I vow that I shall bring you to the throne of the Elysian Empire and that this Aracan Katuvana shall bother Quargard no longer."

Freya blinked away more tears, twisting the seal ring on her finger, "In my brother's name, I swear I shall use all the might of the Empire to bring down the Aracan Katuvana." She sipped her wine and raised the cup, touching it to Lin's.

"I will fulfil my task and bend all my abilities to the removal of the Aracan Katuvana." Kraarz sipped his wine and touched his cup to Lin and Freya's.

"*Oh, so heroic, like something out of a bard's saga.*" Vox said, floating in a circle around the three cups. It flared with white light. "*I imbue these cups with the force of Light. May those who drink from them never tire in their tasks.*" The light surrounded the cups and then faded out.

"To the downfall of the Aracan Katuvana," they said together and drank deeply.

THE JAR TURNED FROM the window to look at the Aracan Katuvana on his throne. The robed figure lay back against his high backed throne, snores sounding from under the hood.

"At last, it begins," the Jar said softly.

Don't miss out!

Visit the website below and you can sign up to receive emails whenever Kira Morgana publishes a new book. There's no charge and no obligation.

https://books2read.com/r/B-A-SVI-OSKPD

BOOKS 2 READ

Connecting independent readers to independent writers.

Did you love *Freya's Freedom*? Then you should read *The Angel's Crown*[1] by Kira Morgana!

[2]

Jenni and Morgana have been forced apart by their parent's divorce. Jenni accompanies their Father to Arkingham, where she finds friends and a life apart from her sister.

Just as she begins to feel comfortable in her new life, the death of her Father's employer brings more than just an uncertain future to rest on her shoulders...

Read more at tpsworld.wordpress.com.

---

1. https://books2read.com/u/3LyOGN

2. https://books2read.com/u/3LyOGN

Also by Kira Morgana

Terrene Empire Tales
Blossom & Kitsune: A Brief Tale of Earthquakes and Nine Tailed Foxes
Snow & Kitsune: A Long Tale of Wild Weather and Tanuki

The Dragon Flower Saga
Hat or Tiara?

The Secret of Arking Down
The Angel's Crown
The Dragon's Pendant
The Second Door

The Tower and The Eye
A Beginning
Party at Castle Grof
Freya's Freedom

Standalone

The Necklace of Harmony: A short story collection

Watch for more at tpsworld.wordpress.com.

About the Author

Kira thought she was a Teacher, until Life pointed out to her that she is actually a writer. As her Cats, Kids and Partner (in that order) approved, she decided to agree with Life.

Currently she is working on a seven book Science Fantasy series, with several accompanying spinoffs and as "A.E. Churchyard" on several Science Fiction projects.

As if that weren't enough to do, she also sings in a Chorus Line, takes Tap lessons, and is delving into the world of Illustration and Graphic Novels

She does all this from a body in South Wales, UK. Where her mind is, she hasn't yet worked out, because apart from seeing a lot of fantasy creatures, she hasn't actually managed to find someone with a connection to a map app...

Read more at tpsworld.wordpress.com.

About the Publisher

Teigr Books is the official Publisher of all Kira Morgana, A. E. Churchyard and Mandy E. Ward books.

www.ingramcontent.com/pod-product-compliance
Lightning Source LLC
Chambersburg PA
CBHW052052150726
48002CB00002B/850